"I'm in personnel for EE&R." Simone was very surprised.

"Dayton, you used to be so skinny in high school! Look at you now!"

Her words tumbled out. She had not expected to see a familiar face.

"You've changed, too, Simone. If I'd known you were going to be this beautiful and this successful, I'd have never let our folks annul our marriage. Do you have time for a glass of sherry? See, I remember your favorite."

"I'm not sure, Dayton." She was reluctant to renew this acquaintance, especially now that she was married…and trying to save that marriage.

Dayton Clark noticed her hesitation.

"Come on, Simone, it's been ten years. We've got to catch up…."

"Well, maybe one glass of sherry would be nice."

LOVE ALWAYS

MILDRED E. RILEY

Genesis Press, Inc.

Indigo

An imprint of Genesis Press, Inc.
Publishing Company

Genesis Press, Inc.
P.O. Box 101
Columbus, MS 39703

All characters in this book have no existence outside the imagination of the author and have no relation whatsoever to anyone bearing the same name or names. They are not even distantly inspired by any individual known or unknown to the author and all incidents are pure invention.

ISBN-13: 978-1-58571-264-9
ISBN-10: 1-58571-264-7
Manufactured in the United States of America

First Edition 1997
Second Edition 2007

Visit us at www.genesis-press.com or call at 1-888-Indigo-1

ACKNOWLEDGMENTS

"Get Here," copyright by Brenda Russell, 1990, from album *Circle of One* by Oleta Adams, London., England, Phonogram, LTD.

To Patterson

PROLOGUE

San Francisco

He drove along, at peace with himself, listening to the hum of the BMW motor. Stopped by a traffic light, he pulled down the visor above the windshield to take a quick look at the picture he had placed there. He smiled. Yes, it would happen soon.

The light changed, and he accelerated smoothly to a comfortable speed. The late afternoon sun flickered through the trees and cast alternating shadows on his face. The sensation of bright light and dark shadows disturbed him, seeming to trigger a mysterious impulse in his brain, so he pushed harder on the gas pedal to flee from the stimuli, checking his rearview mirror for any police car.

She was coming to him. Thank you, Wall Street Week, he thought. How lucky he was to have been watching that particular Friday night when the television program featured the young, vibrant African-American financial analyst. She would be with him in a few days. This time, this time, he would not let her go.

CHAPTER I

Balancing precariously on one foot, Simone struggled with the bulky bags of groceries in each arm but was able to slam the door shut with her foot. She kicked off her high-heeled shoes and leaned against the door with a deep sigh before she gathered enough strength to move. She padded in her stocking feet to her kitchen, where she dropped the awkward bundles on the counter.

She looked over to the cornet. On her tiny mini-desk the flashing light of her answering machine summoned her. How she hated that machine! It was such an intrusive device, but a necessary evil in her life. Of course, she didn't have to respond to it, but if she wanted to stay in business, it was vital. Her clients almost always seemed to need to reach her at once, particularly when it concerned their investments. Of course, she couldn't blame them. People's money was essential to their well-being.

She punched the play button on the machine. As she expected, the first call on the tape was from one of her newest clients. He was feeling a great deal of panic over a slight dip in the market. Simone could hear the stress in his voice as he gave her instructions.

"I want you to sell that computer stock that we talked about earlier. Please, first thing Monday morning, unload all my shares of High Ridge Computer."

Simone shook her head, sat down at the desk, and made a brief note to herself. Her advice to her client had been to stay with the company, but it was his money and she would follow his instructions. She would receive her fee, in any case.

She put away her groceries as she listened to the rest of the message tape. One message was from her mother, calling from Richmond to remind her of the family reunion. "Remember," her mother said, "we're expecting you to plan the activities for the family in Boston. You know, sight-seeing and entertainment. Anyway, call me when you can. Love ya, baby," and her mother rang off.

There was another call, a man's voice that sounded deep and somewhat garbled. She didn't get the name; sounded like a salesman. She'd play it back again later when she had more time.

"Hey, girl!" Her friend Christine's cheerful voice came through the speaker. "Hope you haven't forgotten tonight. We'll be by to pick you up 'round sevenish. Baby, you are going to love Tony Housner, bet on it!"

Simone groaned out loud. Chris and her doctor friends, she thought as she placed string beans, broccoli, and carrots into the vegetable keeper of the refrigerator. Chris was always trying to fix Simone up with some of the doctors she knew at the hospital. Simone thought that Chris had been trying harder since she had become engaged to Warren Conrad, an MIT engineering professor. It seemed to Simone, however, that many of the black doctors Chris introduced her to were so strongly opinionated, so sure of themselves. She found them shallow and insufferable. But Christine Langley was a good friend, and now that she had found the man of her life and was engaged to be married, she was not going to be satisfied until her friend Simone was "fixed up" too.

Simone realized that her own competitive nature put many men off, but she'd been that way all her life. Her mother always said that her middle sibling should have been a boy.

Simone shut off the answering machine and made a cup of tea. She took it into her bedroom and, while she sipped the hot liquid, she wondered what to wear She promised herself she would be a "good girl" tonight, behave herself, and not get anyone's hackles up—so she decided to wear something lady-like and feminine.

She walked to the full-length double mirrors in front of her closet and stared at her reflection. She did not have the distinctive ivory-rose skin of her beautiful mother and her older sister, Cleo. However, she'd been told by many that she was very attractive. She had inherited her coloring from her father, whom she adored.

Her skin was a flawless, smooth, warm brown, and her eyes, large and black, stared back at her. Her thick black hair had been cut short into a modified wedge. Simone always opted for a quick, easy hairstyle, and this present style suited her tendency to spend a limited amount of time on personal grooming and still be professional and well put together. Her small bones and slender body belied her strength and endurance. In high school and college she had run track, and even today she ran whenever she could. Her waiflike appearance refuted her independent nature. She always surprised people with her strong sense of purpose.

She had asked her mother about it. "Momma, is it because I'm a middle child that I'm always so competitive, always trying to outdo and outperform everybody else?"

Her mother had replied patiently, "Child, don't ask me. When you were born, the doctor told me you were an angry baby, fists balled up, so mad, so upset, said you were yelling and screeching to get into this world. He said it looked to him like you were ready to pick a fight with anybody, didn't care who it was," her mother laughed.

"Oh, God, Momma," Simone apologized, hugging her mother. "I hope I haven't been a disappointment to you and Daddy."

"No, honey," her mother embraced her. "Once we got you out of that marriage mess, you've done us proud, and we're happy as can be with your success. Knew you would be okay. Now, if only..."

"I know. If only I'd find the right man and settle down."

She thought about that conversation with her mother, which had taken place when she was home for the Christmas holiday. Would this blind date tonight with Chris and her boyfriend bring a prospective husband into her life? Not that she was actively looking for a mate; but even she realized that, though she had a busy and satisfying life, it was not complete. She was doing well financially, had an attractive apartment and many friends, male and female, but apparently unless she had a "significant other" she was an anomaly—the odd woman out, so to speak, as well as an undefined threat to other singles who were "looking."

She searched her closet. There was that new Carolyn Herrera number she had purchased her last time in New

York. She had been saving it for a special occasion, and that could be tonight. A soft orchid-grey, simple sheath of sheer crepe with an underslip shimmering beneath, it had a high, mandarin-type neckline that framed Simone's small oval face. Sleeveless, it flared slightly at her knees, showing her very attractive legs to an advantage. Simone had been fortunate to find a pair of slender, T-strap sandals and a small bag that exactly matched the shade of her dress. She selected pearl drop earrings, a pearl bracelet with an amethyst clasp, and a large cut amethyst dinner ring as her jewelry. Finally, she those a Hermes scarf in case the air conditioning made the restaurant too cool. The jewel-like colors of orchid, blue, and rose were just elegant enough to complement her dress.

Before showering, Simone prepared a small tray of canapés and hors d'oeuvres and placed a bottle of champagne to chill in an ice bucket. As she explained to Chris when she returned her call confirming the evening out, "Just something so we can have a little chat before we go to dinner. A warm-up, some exploration time. An icebreaker. Whatever you want to call it, Chris. I'd like to get an impression of this blind date you're forcing on me."

"Now, Simone, don't be tough! He's a very nice person. You'll like him, you'll see," Chris reassured her.

As soon as the proper moment presented itself, Simone invited Chris to join her in the kitchen.

"Of course I'll help you. These hors d'oeuvres, especially the stuffed mushrooms, are great, Simone. Where did you find them?" Chris questioned as the two women left the men in the living room.

"A deli down the street," Simone said as she hurried Chris into the kitchen. She closed the door quickly, hugged Chris, and whispered hoarsely, "Chris, he's the handsomest, most distinguished man I've ever seen!"

Her friend grinned back at her. "Didn't I tell you you'd be impressed? And, girlfriend, he's a really nice, sweet guy. You throw that prejudiced nonsense you have about doctors right out of your head! He's different!"

Simone popped another tray of stuffed mushrooms, rolls of bacon stuffed with shrimp, and small bite-sized quiches into the microwave. She turned on the timer and queried her friend.

"What kind of doctor did you say he was?"

"OB-GYN, I believe, but I think he specializes in infertility. High-risk mothers, something like that."

"Bet his patients are crazy 'bout him. Probably worship him. Anyway, so far, I must admit, his personality shows him to be warm and friendly. No airs, no overpowering ego. I must say, Chris, that I like."

The timer went off. Simone retrieved the hors d'oeuvres and arranged them on a serving platter. She picked up the dish as she and Chris moved to the living room.

"Warren says he's brilliant, has a great practice," Chris whispered as they rejoined the men.

Simone put the tray on the coffee table and distributed fresh napkins to her guests.

"Please," she said, indicating the tray, "help yourself. But be careful, these are hot."

"And delicious, too," her guest said, who had been introduced to her as Dr. Tony Housner.

"I'm glad you like them," Simone smiled.

"Wouldn't do to have them too often, you know, high in cholesterol..."

"Certainly, Doctor..."

"Please call me Tony."

"Well, Tony, certainly you don't have to worry about that."

He's so tall and well-built. Wide strong shoulders, slim hips. And I have to admit I'm fascinated by his walnut-brown, smooth skin. And his eyes, Simone thought, they seem to crinkle at the corners when he smiles. They are so dark, so deep set and quiet. When he looks at me, it's as if he can see inside my soul.

Simone sipped her drink and observed him closely as he responded to her query.

"Not so far, but it still pays to be cautious and prudent where health hazards are concerned," he advised. "So I try to be careful, although sometimes it's hard with a busy practice, but I manage to exercise, run every day, that sort of thing."

"Simone ran track in high school and college," Chris told him.

"Great! Do you still run?"

"When I can," she told him. "I find it very helpful to clear my mind."

"Right. Know what you mean. Maybe we can run together sometime."

"I'd like that, Tony."

"This is an absolutely lovely living room, Miss Harper," he went on. "It's so comfortable, so homelike."

"Thanks, I'm glad you like it. Some of the pieces did come from my home. The sofa I had covered with that pale green chintz was my parents' first piece of furniture when they got married. This coffee table," she pointed to a large mahogany-framed, glass-topped long, low coffee table, "belonged to my folks, too. I had to beg for it when they decided to buy new furniture. I was lucky enough to put my bid in before my sister and brother did," she laughed.

"It's a magnificent table. I can see why you would want to have it. The whole room is perfect."

"Thanks, I'm comfortable in it."

Chris spoke up as she placed her empty glass on the table.

"How 'bout it, gang? What say we cut out for the restaurant? Reservations are for seven-thirty, didn't you say, Warren?"

She looked at her fiancé, who gave her a warm smile.

"Not to worry, my love. We do have a seven-thirty reservation, but they will hold it until eight-fifteen," he reassured her. He turned to Simone. "Thanks for the champagne and snacks, Sim. I really needed a little something."

"Oh, you know you're welcome, Warren. Know what you mean. I don't like to be too hungry when I go out to eat. If I'm starved, I tend to eat too fast. I think when you eat out, you should savor the whole experience: the food, the ambience the restaurant offers, the luxury of being waited on, and catered to."

"I can tell you, eating out is something I haven't had the chance to do often," Tony volunteered. "Certainly not in posh places like this Maison Robert where we're going tonight. If I didn't eat at home, it was usually some fast-food joint. When we were medical students and interns, it was grab what you could and keep moving. Never had enough time. Always on duty or on call, or on something," he laughed.

They chuckled at his remarks as they made their way out of Simone's apartment. Just as she closed and was about to lock the door, Simone heard her phone ring.

Tony questioned her, "Do you want to get that?"

Simone shook her head. "No, I left my machine on. I'll check it later when I come home."

"Guess I'm an old fuddy-duddy," Tony said. "I'd be worried it might be one of my patients."

Simone explained, "In my line of work, my clients know nothing happens from four o'clock Friday afternoon until after nine o'clock on Monday morning."

"It's different with me," Tony said as he helped her into the back seat of Warren's Mercedes. "The weekend seems to be when most of the crises occur. Warren says you're a financial consultant. What exactly do you do?"

His question hung in the air between them, but before Simone could say anything in answer, Chris turned around from the front seat to respond.

"She helps people make money, and she's really good at it. Say," she said brightly, "you two people have more in common than you realize." She giggled lightly, "Simone helps people make money, and you help people make families. How about that!"

They all laughed at the comparison as Warren drove skillfully around Boston Common to the old city hall that had been transformed to an elegant French restaurant.

"I suppose there is a common thread in what we do," Simone ventured thoughtfully. "I take a financial history of my prospective clients, then I ask about goals and future plans they may have, to try and get an idea of where they want to be financially ten, fifteen years down the road. I try to come up with an investment plan that I believe will fit their needs."

"Might be a slight similarity in our two lines of work at that," Tony suggested.

"Such as?" Simone questioned.

"Uh huh. I begin with a history-taking procedure as well. Then a medical history and complete physical work-up of each partner. Actually, I have to determine if one or the other or, sadly, both partners are at fault."

"It must be heartbreaking when you have to tell them one or the other has a problem."

"Yes, it is, Miss Harper, but I try to offer hope if I can. Today there are many procedures we can use to help couples with their fertility problems. Every day, research brings new answers. Some are so new that they weren't available five or ten years ago."

Simone felt intrigued by the handsome, well-spoken, friendly man she had been paired with for the evening. An inner voice cautioned her to be careful. She couldn't become impetuous over this Dr. Housner. She'd have to keep both feet on the ground, maintain her composure, and not be swept away by his good looks and charm. That had happened before, and had been a nearly disastrous mistake. She did not intend to make the same mistake again. But she would be pleasant.

"Please," she said to him, "we've been together more than an hour and broken bread at my home. Think you can call me by my first name, Simone?"

"A beautiful name for a beautiful lady," Tony said. "I'd like to call you often, if I may," he grinned at her as he took her hand in his.

"We'll see," Simone murmured. She felt the smooth strength in his fingers as he held her hand. "We'll see."

She allowed a faint hope for the future to rise in her mind as they all entered the restaurant.

CHAPTER II

Having made a decision to relax and enjoy the evening, Simone entered the convivial atmosphere. The maitre d' welcomed them warmly, with an unmistakable accent, and led them to their table. Several waiters hovered with fresh water for their glasses and placed French rolls and croissants on their butter plates. A formally dressed waiter came to take their orders.

Warren Conrad acted as host and gave their orders to the waiter. Each one decided to begin the meal with an order of escargot garlique. Simone decided on a fish entree, salmon, and the two men chose beef. Chris said that broiled chicken would be fine for her.

Their dinner conversation was casual, mainly talk about the changes in the world, both economic and political. Simone noticed that Tony's ideas were practical and forthright, much like her own.

"I'm not too happy with the way the Supreme Court is lining up. You know, Warren?" Tony said.

"Right," Warren agreed as he sliced into his filet mignon.

"Oh, come on now," Chris protested. "Please, let's not get into politics."

"Men do have a tendency to get serious sometimes. But you're right, Chris," Tony remarked, "I, for one, want to hear more about Simone Harper here." He smiled. "Would you like more wine?" he asked Simone as he gestured to the waiter, who hurried over and prepared to fill her glass.

"No more for me," Simone smiled. "But coffee would be nice."

"Right away, madame." The waiter brought a steaming pot of coffee and filled their cups.

After dessert had been served, they lingered over coffee for a few minutes. Simone realized that she was attracted to this handsome, polite, considerate, self-assured, and urbane man she had just met. She gave Chris a raised eyebrow and a slight nod of her head, which meant, "to the little girls' powder room." Chris understood at once. They made their excuses to the men and hurried off.

There was only one other woman in the ladies' lounge, and as soon as she left, Chris turned to Simone. "Well?" she questioned, her face bright with expectations.

Simone clutched her friend's hand and squeezed it. "Chris, you were right this time. He's really fine! I think I'd like to get to know Dr. Tony Housner a little better."

"Simone, you mean it? Oh, girl, it's time to lighten up and put some love in your life."

"Guess you're right, Chris. I've never said anything to you before, but I'm envious of you and Warren. I've seen how he looks at you, and looks out for you. There's not another woman in the world but you, as far as Warren is concerned."

Chris nodded solemnly. "Warren is my life. You'd better believe it. There are times when I have to pinch myself, can't believe it's happened to me."

"Do me a favor," Simone pleaded.

"I know," Chris said quickly, a knowing grin on her face, "you want some time alone with Tony Housner. Don't worry, kid, follow my lead. Your good friend Chris will fix everything."

Chris didn't take long. As soon as they returned to the table, she spoke right up.

"I don't like to break up this wonderful evening, but I'm on duty at the hospital. Tony, you and Simone don't have to leave."

Tony spoke quickly, "I'll see that Simone gets home safely." He turned to her, "If that's all right with you."

"That would be fine."

Chris explained apologetically, "When you're a head nurse like I am, you have to work your share of weekends—and this is one of my weekends."

She and Simone kissed each other goodbye, and the men shook hands.

"Call me," Chris mouthed to Simone as she and Warren left.

"They're a great couple," Tony observed as he sat down. He signaled again for a waiter.

"They really are. Chris and I were at Boston University together as freshmen, and we've been friends ever since. She says you've known Warren since school days, too."

"Right. We were undergrads together. Then he went to engineering school, and I went to medical school. But, Simone, I want to hear about you. Ah, here we are," he acknowledged as the waiter set down the drinks Tony had ordered.

Tony raised his glass in Simone's direction and offered a toast. "To the most beautiful dinner companion I have ever met and I am hoping for many, many more meetings. To you, lovely Simone."

Simone accepted his toast with a smile. Funny, she had prepared herself to dislike this blind date, but instead there was a sincere warmth to this man that had thrown the stereotypical "blind-date-opinionated-doctor" thinking right out of her mind.

She looked at him over the rim of her glass as she sipped her drink, realizing that what fascinated her most about the man was his eyes. They were dark brown and deep set, but softened by thick, straight, dark eyebrows that shaded them. But his eyes were penetrating, as if he could examine her heart, her soul, every facet of her being. Despite that, they were not cold, but warm and discerning eyes—and Simone sensed that this man, if he cared for someone, would care deeply.

Much of Simone's success with her clients lay in her ability to focus her attention on them. Somehow she could tap into their wishes and goals with skillful questions that helped her to help them succeed. She knew that she had to learn more about Tony Housner.

It was almost as if he'd read her mind.

"Say, Simone," he asked her suddenly, "how would you like to go over to the Hatchery, a jazz club favorite of Harvard students?"

"I'd love it, Tony."

"I've got a friend—well, really, his wife was my patient—who might be able to get us in. He's on the staff there. I believe Oleta Adams is appearing."

"Oleta Adams! One of my favorites! When she sings 'Get Here' I almost melt. Do you think we can make it?"

"I believe we can," he glanced at his watch, "if we leave right now."

That proved not to be easy to accomplish. As Tony and Simone moved toward the front of the restaurant, several patrons recognized him, called out "Dr. Tony" to him, and plucked at his coat sleeve as he moved or reached out to shake his hand.

As Simone watched the warm pleasantries being exchanged, she thought, maybe this man is too good, too perfect. Careful now in her intimate relationships, she knew she had to be cautious and not make another mistake.

"Sorry about that, Simone," Tony said as he hurried to join her. "Some of those people were former patients, success stories. I had to move quickly before some of them hauled out pictures of Junior or Sis," he laughed.

"Must make you feel good, knowing you've helped them."

"It does." He handed a few bills to the parking attendant. "We need a taxi, please."

"Yes, sir. Right away." He whistled, and a nearby taxi pulled up to the curb in front of Tony and Simone.

"To the Hatchery in Cambridge," Tony instructed the driver.

"Tony, these are great seats," Simone observed as they squeezed in behind a tiny table about four rows from the stage. "How did you manage this?"

He grinned at her. "One of my former patients came through."

"Boy, you know everybody, seems to me. Have they all been patients of yours?"

Tony laughed. "Not really all. Some of their wives, maybe."

"Well, you know what I mean, Mr. Smarty," Simone countered.

"Didn't mean to be coy, Simone, but I hope I have made friends with some of the families I've tried to help. Not all, but some."

They stopped conversing because just then the guest artist appeared to loud and enthusiastic applause.

There was no denying the grace and style of the singer-pianist. Her warm, sultry voice, the nuances, the shading of notes and tones she employed reached out to her receptive audience, and every person in the room was enthralled.

Simone glanced at Tony. He, too, was enjoying the singer's talent. Simone couldn't tell when it had happened, but she became aware that Tony's firm, strong hand was holding hers. And it felt right to her. Still, she warned herself, go slow, Simone, go slow. When she withdrew her hand from Tony's to join the applause for the artist, she replaced it in her lap. Seemingly, he did not notice.

When Oleta Adams began singing again, Tony put his arm around Simone's shoulder and sang into her ear, along with the artist, "Get here, get here if you can. There are mountains between us, always something to get over. If I had my way, you would be closer." As the song ended Simone turned to look at him, and in the dim room, without hesitation, Tony kissed her lightly on the lips. To keep her composure, Simone leaned back in her chair, but the feeling of his strong mouth on hers lingered. With others in the room, she joined in applauding the singer.

Oleta Adams accepted the applause with a gracious bow and made an announcement.

"This next song is from my latest album and I hope that you will like it. It's called 'Have You Listened to My Heart.'"

Simone figured from the title that the song should be a blues number, but it turned out to be an upbeat rendition—a woman telling her lover that her heart is his and his only, and if he listened to its message, he would know that she would always love him.

With a final crescendo of chords, the singer's last note died away to thunderous applause. She acknowledged her audience with a nod and a charming smile on her lovely face before leaving the stage.

An aura of warm, hopeful excitement filled the room as people pushed back their chairs to leave. They smiled at each other, murmuring their pleasure at having shared the exciting event.

Tony walked behind Simone through the crowd, with both his hands on her shoulders. She felt the heat and strength of his fingers and wondered what it would feel like to have those hands on more intimate parts of her body. Involuntarily, she shivered.

Tony noticed her reaction at once.

"Are you chilly, Simone?" he asked anxiously.

"No, not really. Think someone walked across my grave, that's all."

"Well, we'll have none of that nonsense," Tony said firmly. "Wait here in the lobby; I'll grab a taxi and we'll get you home."

"I hope we can get together again really soon, Simone," Tony said as the taxi sped across the Charles River toward Boston. "It turned out to be an evening to remember. At least it was for me," he added.

"It was lovely, Tony. Really nice. I may as well confess something to you, if you haven't already guessed it."

"Yes, what?"

"I've never enjoyed blind dates before, but tonight with you proved to be an exception. I had a great time."

"So you wouldn't mind if we get together again? Please say yes, Simone, and let's make it soon. You know, you are an enchanting person, and I do want to know you better."

Simone agreed with a nod and looked out the car window.

At that moment they were passing the First Church of Christ, Scientist, on Massachusetts Avenue. Simone looked at the reflecting pool in front of the majestic building and wished that somehow her own life could be as serene.

Tony noticed her interest in the unusual display of lights and water. He asked her, "Have you ever visited the Mapparium there?"

"Many times, Tony. It's a fascinating exhibition. I'm told people from all over come to visit it and walk inside the glass globe marked with a map of the world."

"I know. Some of my patients are from out of town, and quite often I encourage them to do a bit of sight-seeing while they're in town. You know, to relax, get their minds off themselves. The Mapparium is one of the sites I suggest."

"Does it help them? I mean, to sightsee, that sort of thing?"

"Sometimes I believe it does. Perhaps it's because they relax better, knowing that they are taking some steps to deal with their infertility problem. Who really knows? It does seem to take the edge off some of their anxiety. But let's talk about Simone Harper. I've never known a financial analyst. Tell me more about yourself."

"There's not much…the usual. You know, born in Richmond…my parents are still there. Dad retired as a high school principal, and Mom, well, she's still the most beautiful matron in the city. I have a married brother and a married sister. I came to Boston to go to school and…here I am."

"And I'm glad, 'here I am,' " Tony said. His eyes sought hers in the dim light from the street lamps they passed. The flickering lights flirted enticingly with Simone's attractive face, and he was compelled to reach for her hands.

"Your hands are cold, Simone. Sure you're not coming down with something? You were shivering when we left the Hatchery."

"Oh, I feel fine," she hastened to reassure him. "And, Tony, it's been a great evening. Tell the cab driver it's about half a block down this street," she pointed.

"Number 205, half a block, sir," Tony told the driver.

When they pulled up, Tony dismissed the driver after he paid him.

Um-m-m, Simone thought, how's he going to get home?

As if he had read her mind, Tony announced, "We're practically neighbors, you know. I live in a brownstone about two blocks from here. I can walk home."

Simone drew in a deep breath as they walked into her building. Dare she ask him in for a nightcap? Was she ready for further involvement with this man whom she felt drawn to?

She handed him the key to her apartment door. He unlocked it and gave the key back to her. Then he stepped aside and waited. Simone realized that she had come to a crossroad. Quickly, impulsively, she made up her mind.

"Could you...would you...like to come in...for coffee?" she said.

"That would be nice, if it's not too much trouble," Tony smiled agreeably.

"No trouble. Come in."

Tony watched as Simone put her scarf and bag on the sofa table. He was really intrigued by this tiny wisp of a girl who, nevertheless, appeared to be quite self-sufficient.

"Have a seat," she told him. "Coffee will be ready in a minute."

Tony sat down and looked around. A moderate-sized photograph of a middle-aged, attractive couple rested on the table behind the sofa. He could see that the man resembled Simone. The woman was beautiful, a very attractive matron with short, silver hair. Simone's parents, Tony surmised. Other pictures were there as well, of other family members.

As he looked around the room, he thought he heard a male voice. Then he realized that it must be Simone's answering machine. Evidently she was checking her messages while preparing the coffee.

She appeared with a tray holding two cups of steaming coffee. "I remembered that you took yours black. That okay?"

"Oh, right. You know after years of medical school and internship, it's black coffee."

As he took the cup she handed him, he noticed a distinct pallor in her face, and her hands trembled.

"Are you all right, Simone? I heard you checking your answering machine. No bad news, I hope."

"Just a client panicking over today's drop in the market," she explained. "It was off only a few points, but the fainthearted clients scare easily."

"Sure you're okay?" Tony persisted.

"Of course I'm sure," Simone answered testily, anger rising in her voice. "Why are you questioning me?"

"Don't forget, I'm a doctor, my dear, and I'm accustomed to checking my patients' emotions and welfare..."

Simone raised her eyebrows and glared at Tony.

"Since when did I become one of your patients?" she snapped at him.

"'I just meant..."

"I know what you meant, Doctor. I'm quite capable of taking care of my own welfare and emotions. You're like all the other black, chauvinistic doctors I've met. You think you know everything!"

Stunned, Tony flushed to a deep burgundy hue. What had he said to cause this outburst?

"I...I...I only wanted to be helpful...show my concern," he started to say, but Simone's eyes sparkled with anger. She put her coffee cup on the table, walked to the door, and flung it open.

"You can be helpful by leaving my home," she said.

Tony rose from his seat and walked to the door, his eyes never leaving her face. He leaned over and gave her a kiss on her cheek as she tried to avert her head.

"I'll call you in a few days to see how you're doing," he said softly. "Sorry it had to end like this. It was an unforgettable evening. Good night, Simone."

Simone did not answer; she merely closed the door and locked it. Leaning against it, she quivered with anger—but not anger directed at Tony Housner. The garbled voice on her machine was that of Dayton Clark, the last person on earth she wanted to hear from.

CHAPTER III

On Saturday morning, Simone telephoned her mother in Richmond.

"Yes, Mother, it's me. Want you to know that I've picked out a hotel in Cambridge, near Harvard University. Of course it's nice," she said in response to her mother's inquiry. "Yes, they did give me a special room rate. Why not, Mother, with people coming from all over the country? And what I plan to do is fax you the itinerary so you can have copies made to mail out to everyone. Well, we'll have a bus for sight-seeing trips and, yes, they will accommodate Aunt Emma and the rest of the older folks."

Her mother gave her more instructions, to which Simone agreed. "Oh, yes, I'll keep in touch about all the details. Tell Dad I said hi."

After she reassured her mother that she was well and doing fine, to her mother's complaint, "My baby up there in Boston, all by herself," Simone hung up with the promise to keep her mother, as chairwoman of the Harper family reunion, aware of all the details.

Then she turned to clean up after last night. She'd been too upset to clear away the dirty glasses, soiled napkins, and coffee cups from the night before. She went to the living room, gathering everything on a tray. There was the half-full coffee cup Tony had been drinking from when she had unceremoniously thrown him out of her apartment.

She washed and dried the champagne glasses and put them away, then the cups and saucers.

Damn that Dayton, she thought. What makes him think he can come back into my life? And why would I be interested? As she remembered, the boy had always been so presuming. Like last night. "Mone, I'll be in Boston on business for a few days. Like to look you up, see how you're doing. I'll give you a call when I'm in town."

Dayton's voice had sounded strange to her. After all, it had been more than ten years. At twenty-eight, she was not the stupid, naive girl she was at eighteen. Their elopement on prom night was just that: a foolish, impetuous escapade. Thank God her folks were able to have it annulled. And Dayton Clark did not interest her now, that was for sure.

But the man she met last night, Tony Housner—now she was interested in him.

In the clear light of morning, she felt ashamed at the way she had railed against him. What was the matter with her? She wouldn't have believed that hearing from someone from her past, like Dayton, could upset her so. After all these years of dealing with her clients' finances, understanding and advising them on the vagaries of the stock market, surely she could deal with something as innocuous as a teenage elopement. Perhaps, she reckoned, that was why she was upset. Dayton reminded her of a failure in her life, and it bothered her. She hated to fail.

During the next hour she straightened up the apartment, getting rid of an accumulation of magazines and newspapers for the recycling bin. Then she examined some bills to be paid, wrote out the checks, and stamped the envelopes. She'd drop them in the mail later.

Her mind kept reviewing the evening she had spent with her friends. Tony Housner kept crowding into her thoughts.

She touched her face gingerly, as if it had been marked by the gentle kiss he had brushed against her cheek on leaving. Her face flushed at the memory. Her behavior was not at all that of the sophisticated, cosmopolitan business-woman she liked to project.

Perhaps some strenuous exercise would dear her head. With her favorite exercise video in the VCR, five minutes had passed when the telephone interrupted her routine.

She hesitated before answering; then, remembering that the answering machine was not on, she quickly shut off the tape and ran to pick up the receiver in the kitchen. It was only a few steps from her bedroom to the kitchen, but she breathed a fluttery hello into the mouthpiece.

"Hel...hello," she breathed.

"Hi, Simone, Tony Housner here."

"Oh, hi, Tony."

"I hope I haven't reached you at a bad time. You sound out of breath."

"Exercising."

"Ah, sorry 'bout that. I know people hate to be inter-rupted..."

"It's all right."

"I wanted to see how you were feeling."

"I'm fine, Tony."

"Great, I'm glad. The other thing I wanted to ask is, would you like to join me for Sunday morning brunch—tomorrow morning, that is? They have an outstanding brunch at the Barton Hotel at Copley Square, with a fantastic gospel choir that really rocks the place. How about it? Would you like to go?"

Quickly Simone realized that Tony had not mentioned her outburst of the night before. Had he forgotten about it, she wondered? An apology for her behavior was on the tip of her tongue. She started to speak, then thought, he's not upset over it and wants to see me again, so she accepted his invitation.

"Yes, Tony, I would like to join you."

"Perfect. Pick you up at ten, okay?"

"Fine. See you then."

"I'll be ready." She hung up the phone.

Intuitively, Tony realized that something unusual had upset Simone. After hearing the telephone messages, her whole persona had changed. How could he help her? There was no doubt in his mind that he had to help her, because finally he had met the woman he wanted to marry.

Simone was small, but deceptively strong—a fact he had noticed when they first met. When she shook hands with him, her grasp was not masculine hard, but firm and sure. And when she looked at him, there was no wavering in her glance—only direct eye contact. He recalled the delicate scent of her perfume when he had held her dose while they listened to Oleta Adams. The fascinating mix of hardy independence and elegant style made him want to seek a more permanent relationship. He remembered other women in his life—some from his college days, others from his busy years in medical school—but none had ever made him want a deeper commitment. At last, he had found the only one he wanted his mother to meet.

Around noon that day, Simone received another call. It was Chris.

"Had to call you, girl, find out what's goin' on," she said, her voice bright with curiosity.

"Well," Simone dragged the phrase out slowly, "not too much. Having brunch with Tony tomorrow morning."

Chris screeched over the phone. "Not too much! Not too much!"

Simone moved the telephone a few inches from her ear. Chris was really excited.

"Girl, what do you mean, 'not too much'?" she echoed Simone's limp response. "Going to have brunch! That's a start. Where?"

"Down Copley Square. The new Barton Hotel."

"Oh my gawd, one of the most expensive in town! You're going to love it! I understand they have everything on the menu from caviar to fried oysters to roast beef to a fish delicacy, finnan haddie. You name it, they serve it. Seems to me that Tony Housner is serious..."

"Well, maybe..." Simone said, caution reflected in her tone of voice. Chris picked up on her friend's mood immediately.

"I don't know about you, Simone. Don't sound too enthusiastic to me. What's the matter with you?"

Simone knew Chris would not let up until she worried the problem out of her. Maybe it was just as well that she share it with her.

"Dayton Clark called me last night," she announced.

"Dayton Clark? Who's Dayton Clark?"

"Some guy from my past. We eloped when I was eighteen."

"Oh, *that* Dayton Clark! I remember, you told me about it. What'd he want?"

"Said he'd be in town for a few days, wants to see me, touch base for old times' sake."

Practical as always, Chris reminded Simone, "There's no law that says you have to see him…besides, what for?"

"For some kind of ending to the situation. Our parents separated us that day, and…"

"Simone, all of that happened in the past, and it belongs there in the past. You know that. Now, on to more important things. Tell me about you and Tony. What did you guys do after Warren and I left?"

"Went over to Cambridge to the Hatchery. Oleta Adams was singing."

"Simone! You lucky dog! One of my favorites."

"Mine too."

"Then what? Don't leave out *anything!* I want to hear the whole story."

"Nothing else. He brought me home, we had coffee, and…he left."

"Oh no, don't try to con me, Simone Harper. I know something happened. I can hear it in your voice. You don't have to tell me now. I'm coming by after I get off duty. I expect you to fill me in then. Completely! Bye."

Simone hung up the phone. She knew that Chris would never rest until she heard the whole story. Her silly fight with Tony and everything. It was probably her Wampanoug Indian heritage that gave her friend her strong, practical nature and the pragmatism that first attracted Simone to the tall, athletically built, no-nonsense young woman. The two were opposites. Simone, quick and mercurial, was like a flash of silver, while Chris was methodical and pedantic. She never made a move without planning for the outcome. She had high cheekbones and heavy, thick, dark-brown hair from her Indian ancestry, as well as the red-brown tones in her skin coloring.

Simone treasured their friendship, and was delighted when they renewed it on Chris' return to Boston after completing her master's degree in psychiatric nursing at Yale. Chris was wise and unflappable, traits that helped her deal with the daily crises in her patients' lives.

CHAPTER IV

It was the first time Simone had seen Tony in the daytime. His good looks almost took her breath away. He arrived at her apartment promptly at ten. The sky was a breathtakingly clear blue, with hardly a wisp of a cloud, and the air was soft and warm. It was one of Boston's bright, sunny mornings.

Tony wore white slacks, with a crisp blue shirt open at the neck.

"I have a bow-tie in my pocket so I'll look proper when we go in to eat," he explained to Simone.

His sport coat was a sunflower-yellow linen, which enhanced his bronze good looks. The sun also brought out the silver glints in his hair at the temples. Simone noticed, too, that there was warmth and a sparkle in Tony's eyes when he looked at her.

She was glad she had worn her raspberry silk jumpsuit. She was certain the color was perfect for her cinnamon soft skin. She realized it picked up the color of the lipstick and makeup that she wore. She was pleased by the appreciative, low whistle Tony gave when he saw her.

All at once, Friday night's episode was in the past, and Simone made up her mind to enjoy herself. Tony's hand was firm and warm on her elbow as he helped her down the stairs and into his car. Tony Housner knew how to make a woman feel special. She liked that.

The brunch was everything Chris had said it would be. The dining room was bright and colorful. In front of the long table with assorted dishes, a path of terracotta pots filled with geraniums guided the guests to the various entrees.

Simone settled for a fresh fruit compote, french toast with honey, a green salad, and a serving of chicken on rice. A tall glass of orange juice and fresh coffee were her choices for beverages.

"You don't eat much, Simone," Tony observed as he dug into his plate of roast beef, rice, salad, and assorted rolls and muffins. "I've already run five miles this morning, so I'm ready to load up."

"Where do you usually run?" Simone asked.

"Most times I drive over to the Arborway, park the car, and run around Jamaica Pond. What about you? Where do you usually run?"

"I've been over to Jamaica Pond. Funny we've never met. And sometimes I've been to Hammond Pond in Newton, but my favorite is the high school track that was built for the famous basketball star."

"I know," Tony said solemnly as he drank some of his orange juice. "The one who left money in his trust to do something for the inner-city kids."

"Jerry Caldwell, that was his name," Simone remembered.

"Right. Well, perhaps we can run together at Caldwell Arena. It's open to the public."

"Yes, it is, Tony. It's a nice track, built so that it's easy to run on. Not too hard, packed—cushioned just right."

"I'd like to try it sometime. Oh, Simone, the choir..."

He was interrupted by the appearance of several men and women dressed in green and gold choir robes. They came in singing, with their healthy, boisterous voices filling the room. A small portable organ had been moved to one corner of the room, and the singers—four women and five men of varying ages—took their places around it.

Hands clapped in time to the vigorous sounds, and Simone found herself tapping her foot and moving in her chair to the music. She looked at Tony. His face was luminous with delight, and he sang along with the choir.

"Reminds me of church back home," Simone whispered when the number ended.

"Sure does, Simone."

"Did you sing in a church choir, Tony?" Simone questioned, her eyes focused on his fascinating mouth as she remembered the warm, sensitive feeling of his lips on hers. Was it only thirty-six hours since they'd met?

Tony had been watching Simone closely, too. He hoped she had gotten over that earlier disturbance when she abruptly asked him to leave Friday. Whatever it was, he hoped it was behind her. He loved seeing her bright smile and her obvious enjoyment of their outing. He was bewitched by her sensuous mouth; her full, berry-wine lips enticed him. He remembered the first brief taste he had savored last Friday night at the jazz dub. When would he have a chance to relive that kiss?

During the choir's next number, the singers walked around the room, shaking hands and inviting those who could to join in their gospel hymn.

Tony sang with a deep bass voice. Apparently he knew the hymn "Ride on King Jesus," and his voice added a timbre to the other voices that caused smiles all around.

Simone grinned at him when the hymn was finished.

"You answered my question, Tony. You did sing in the church choir! You have a marvelous voice."

"Thanks, Simone. I love music. Part of my heritage, I think."

"I'm crazy about good music, too," she informed him, "but I'm one of those people of color who can't carry a tune!"

"That's fine with me, Simone. You have plenty of other assets to delight the senses," he laughed.

"Tony, my office is not too far away. On Fremont Street, really. Would you mind driving me over? I need to pick up a few fact sheets to look over before tomorrow."

"I'd love to take you, Simone. Lead the way, after I get the check."

Her office was located on the fifth floor of an office building overlooking the Boston Common. Simone had several keys for the building, the elevator, and her own suite of offices.

After entering the building, she punched in the code for the security.

"Can't be too careful," she told Tony.

"That's true," he concurred. "We are very careful with our security measures at the hospital," he told her.

He followed her to an office door. A sign on the wall read *Simone Harper, Financial Services Consultant.*

When Simone unlocked the door and stepped aside to let Tony enter, he did so, and his first words were, "Wow, look at this!"

Simone smiled as she watched his reaction. She could see that Tony was impressed.

"Simone, this is really elegant."

Her office reflected her personality. The walls were covered with a fabric of gold and deep orchid, with splashes of muted orange tones. It was furnished with glass-topped metal desks and tables; Italian leather sofas and chairs were tastefully arranged around a modern gas-fired fireplace. The total ambiance gave clients and visitors a sense of elegant comfort.

"When clients come to me," Simone ticked off the items with her fingers, "they must feel, see, and taste success. Heavy wooden furniture and paneling smack too much of the old-fashioned way of doing things, you know. Quite a few of my clients are unaccustomed to having personal advisors, and I like to put them at ease, if I can."

Tony looked at Simone. His appraisal of her had not been wrong. She was smart and clever. He looked at her framed degrees on the wall, plus several citations that indicated Simone's community involvement. There was a picture of her with several young boys in baseball uniforms. He picked it up. Simone was standing in the back row, a wide grin on her face.

"My little league team that I sponsor," she said. "We came in second in the league."

"Goodness, there's no end to your talent, girl," Tony said.

"I told you I was a tomboy, didn't I?" she teased.

"And a mighty attractive one, is all I can say," Tony grinned back at her.

"I think what I want may be here in my secretary's desk," Simone said as she checked several drawers of a corner desk. "Nope, not here. Well," she said to Tony, "now you'll get to see my office. This way, sir," and she walked ahead of him down a short, carpeted hall that led to her office.

Tony was charmed by the effervescence of Simone's quicksilver personality. He was accustomed to the cerebral, pedantic life of medicine, and Simone's practical, no-nonsense approach appealed to him. As he followed her—her proud walk, with her head held high; the spirited energy that seemed to enliven her, at this moment, in her own milieu.

Tony felt himself enthralled by this unusual person. He had almost given up on finding her, this young woman whom he had known for only two days, but he felt he had always known and loved her. Was it supposed to happen like this, in this day and age? he wondered.

Simone's inner sanctum was not as decorative as her reception room. A large functional desk with a computer, fax machine, and other electronic devices figured prominently in the room. Behind the desk was a comfortable chair that could be swiveled to look out a huge window onto Boston Common. The room was light, airy and practical.

"This is where I really get down to business, Tony. Have a seat," she indicated a chair to the right of her desk, "while I look for those fact sheets. Connie, my secretary, is usually very good...aha, here they are."

She put the sheets in an 8x10 envelope and stood up.

"Ready?" she questioned Tony.

Tony looked at her. What he saw was a small-boned, fragile-appearing, beautiful, tawny-faced woman who simply mesmerized him.

He shook his head as if coming out of a trance.

"Ready? Ready for what, Simone?"

"Ready to leave," she said. "I've got what I came for, so we can go now."

Tony looked out the window. He didn't want to leave just yet.

"You have a great view, Simone."

Simone joined him and stood beside him. Her head barely reached his shoulder. At six-feet-four, Tony could have been a star basketball player. But his dream was a medical career, so he limited his ball playing to shooting hoops with friends. Standing there beside Simone, sharing the view of the Common with her, it seemed to him that his whole life—basketball, medicine, his career—paled in comparison to this moment. He turned to Simone.

"Simone." His voice was ragged with emotion. Her eyes met his. Neither of them spoke. There was no need. The air in the quiet room was filled with expectancy. Simone knew the moment she had waited for had arrived. Her eyes met Tony's, and what he saw in them gave him the permission he sought. He bent to kiss her, and her lips met his with such an eager hunger that Simone's whole body quivered.

Tony's arms tightened around her as his mouth sought to conquer hers. His lips were soft and mobile, yet strong and firm. Simone yielded to the sweet sensation as Tony's tongue reached to taste her sweetness. She reached up to cradle his noble head in both hands as Tony continued to kiss her eyes, her cheeks, her neck.

"Simone," Tony moaned into the soft crevice between her neck and shoulder. His hand cupped her breast, and his fingers moved seductively over the sensitive bud beneath her silk blouse. Simone responded to Tony's caresses with a soft moan of her own. Her hunger for Tony was escalating, and she realized that unless she did something right now, there would be no turning back. Like a child searching for a safe haven, Simone knew she was where she wanted to be: in Tony Housner's arms.

She could feel his strong, lean body pressed close to hers, the strong length of his muscular thighs, and the unmistakable urgency of his masculine arousal. For Simone, the world stood still. She had no thought of yesterday or tomorrow, only this moment in Tony's arms was real to her.

Their breathing was the only sound in the room; the sounds of traffic outside seemed muted and far away.

Tony had reached the row of buttons at the back of Simone's blouse. He unbuttoned them while still claiming her mouth with his own. Suddenly, he scooped her up in his arms. He had remembered the Italian leather sofa in her reception room. He carried her there and laid her gently on the soft leather. It was quiet in that room; they could have been isolated on a far-away island. Simone watched Tony as he released her blouse from her shoulders and pulled it to her waist. She leaned forward with both her hands on his shoulders so he could unclasp her bra. When her softly rounded breasts were revealed, Tony moaned and bent forward to kiss them. Simone had kicked off her sandals and felt her bare toes curl as Tony nipped and savored first one breast, then the other. She struggled and pulled to help Tony out of his coat and shirt, which he threw on a nearby chair. Then he loosened her slacks at her waistline. Simone raised her hips so that Tony could pull them down. Soon there was a pool of raspberry-colored silk on the floor beside them.

"My God, Simone," Tony's voice rasped with taut emotion, "you are so beautiful!" He looked down on her incredulously, as if he had created her and was astonished by his own handiwork. Simone opened her arms to welcome him, and he sighed in complete gratification as he tasted first one roseate bud of her breast, then the other. She felt as if her body would melt away into nothingness. Tony raised her head from her bosom to claim her mouth with searing kisses.

"Simone?" he whispered into her mouth.

She shook her head wildly and murmured, "Yes, Tony, yes! Now!" she insisted.

She watched as Tony reached with his long arm into the jacket of his coat pocket and pulled out a foil-wrapped packet.

"Never want to hurt you, my love," he whispered. "I love you too much."

Simone's eyes squeezed soft tears as she realized the great consideration and care Tony was showing her. She reached for the security of his mouth again and held his head close while she kissed him with a hunger she didn't know she possessed.

Tony stroked the velvety skin of her slender thighs and her small, taut abdomen. His fingers feathered the downy triangle between her legs, and Simone writhed in anticipation. She was moving inexorably toward the culmination of a moment that she knew would change her life.

"Tony," she whispered. Her plea reached him, and he held her in his arms. Without any will of her own, her legs wrapped themselves around Tony, and she sensed him moving steadily toward her. The moisture she felt surprised her as she moved her hips seductively to accommodate him. He was gentle but demanding as he entered her slowly. Then suddenly he began to move deep inside her. She responded with a moving cadence of her own that matched his. Their bodies continued to move until they soared into a far-away apex of delight as a thunderous roar sprang from Tony's throat. He shuddered from the explosion that had gripped him.

"My beautiful, wonderful Simone," he said softly as he lay spent, his head on her breasts.

Simone allowed the tears to slide slowly down her cheeks as she held his head close. She could feel his pulse still racing as his breathing slowed. She had not believed that happiness would come to her like this.

CHAPTER V

Simone filled her days with her clients and their financial needs. She was extremely busy and had been invited to participate with other financial consultants in workshops around metropolitan Boston. She and Tony had become an item, to the delight of Chris.

They loved the evenings that they shared whenever Tony had relief from the hospital. Simone, always perfectly groomed, wore her clothes with the ease and confidence of a professional model. Tony was proud of her looks. Her tawny-brown coloring and large black eyes framed by thick, sable-black hair that was cut to graze softly toward her lovely cheekbones made him catch his breath. Her small frame was complemented by the silver-greys, greens, and jewel-toned colors that she preferred.

Tony told her once when they were dancing, "I never knew that anyone as tiny as you could be so elegant and perfect. Having you in my arms makes me feel like the richest man in America."

Simone smiled and snuggled closer, her head on his chest.

After weeks into their relationship, when it became obvious to them that they were irrevocably attracted to each other, Simone revealed to Tony the story of her disastrous teenage marriage.

"What did I know then, Tony?" she asked. Remembering, she continued quietly.

"It was an idea born of boredom, a need for adventure. It was prom night, and this boy and I went over the state line and got married. I thought I was discovering for the first time a world that no one had ever known, the world of true love."

She looked up at him and touched his face. "I know better now, Tony," she said.

He hugged her close. "What happened?" he wanted to know.

"We were so dumb, so naive. We went back home and told our folks. They had fits, both his folks and mine. They had the marriage annulled. We were both too young."

"And now..."

"And now, I know what I'm doing. I'm not too young."

Tony and Simone's marriage took place at Boston University's Marsh Chapel. Members of each family were present. Tony's older brother, Bart, had come from New Jersey to serve as best man, and Simone's married sister, Cleo, had flown from Richmond to be matron of honor. Friends from their respective colleges and some of Tony's medical colleagues and hospital staff attended the gala affair.

Simone wore a gown of eggshell-ivory satin. Her train of gossamer organza provided a cloud-like illusion as she walked toward Tony at the altar, seeming almost weightless. The pearl and gold earrings that Tony had given her as a wedding gift added to her regal appearance. Tony's eyes filled with tears as he looked at the paradoxically fragile but strong young woman about to become his wife. A fleeting wave of anxiety passed over him, but he felt a breathless eagerness to move past the moment, to see what would be around the corner in his life with this woman he loved.

Earlier that morning, his widowed mother had found him in his bedroom. She had kissed him, held him tightly for a moment, and looked up into her tall son's face, searching for reassurance.

"Tony, are you sure?" Her eyes glistened.

"Oh, Mom, of course I'm sure," he had answered quickly. He gave her a warm squeeze. She knew he meant to be comforting and to allay her doubts, but she wasn't at all sure of this marriage. Her son had waited a long time to marry; he was thirty-four, and she wanted him to be happy.

His mother would have worried more if she had known that this was Simone's second marriage.

The couple was able to take a three-day weekend trip to Jamaica before they returned to Tony's brownstone condominium in Boston's South End. Anxious to redecorate her new home, Simone agreed to wait until Tony was more secure in his profession. In a transitional period in his career, he was negotiating to become a staff physician at Pioneer Women's Hospital. As a member of the staff, he could utilize the hospital's facilities, laboratories, and clinics to further his research in human reproductive infertility.

Sexually, Tony and Simone were very compatible. When he came home from work, Tony never knew whether Simone would be in a bubble bath, ready to invite him to join her, or would greet him at the door in an African Kente cloth robe and matching turban, or perhaps wearing a sleek robe…or only a large bath towel that she'd whip off the minute the front door closed, throwing herself into his open arms. She was like a delightful child at times, and Tony was enchanted by her.

Only six months into the marriage, however, the frenetic pace began to wear on Tony. Simone belonged to many social groups, alumni associations, and networking and business groups. Although constantly involved in activities outside the home, she seemed to glow with the pace of endless parties and nightlife. Once, when Tony objected to some cocktail affair that they were dressing for, she told him, "It's important for me to socialize, to be seen, and to be able to network…you know, meet potential clients. I should think it would be important for you, too," she said as she slipped her dress over her head and turned her back to him for help with the zipper.

"Well, maybe," he replied grudgingly, "but most of my patients are referred to me by other doctors."

He sighed and patted her lightly on her backside. She looked great in her little black dress. As usual, he knew she would have a good time, but he was getting tired of all the parties…and the people.

Although Simone had attended undergraduate school in Boston, her childhood home was Richmond, Virginia, where her parents still lived. Her Southern upbringing, she said, meant that family, friends, and just "plain ole people" were very important in her life. Sometimes she would fall back into some down-home saying from her childhood, such as "You got to lay them bricks straight, chile, 'cause you may have to walk back on over them." She could be sophisticated one moment and in the next instant a small-town country girl. She constantly surprised Tony.

"Simone," Tony said one morning at breakfast, "we've got to have some down time at home. I'm just not able to go out every evening. I have some extra reading I've got to do, and..."

"I know, I know," she interrupted. "Our pace has been rather fast. Okay. This weekend, let's see," she picked up the calendar from the kitchen counter, "nothing going on except for my sorority dinner dance. We can skip that."

"No, certainly not," Tony said. "You're the chairperson of the committee, and you've worked hard on that—but sometime soon, let's plan time to be at home."

But they never did. Simone was so involved that she couldn't break off her many commitments. When they were home on a rare weekend, they were not together. Tony would be in his den, reading medical journals, and Simone would be on the phone, "networking," as she called it, with one of her friends. They never seemed to be with each other except for meals and in bed. Most often, they ate carryout meals picked up by one or the other on the way home. To Tony's dismay, Simone was not a cook and showed no motivation to learn.

As a busy physician, Tony Housner needed quiet moments after hectic days in the clinic. The emotional trauma he felt after dealing with couples desperate for a child drained him.

"Leave it at the front door," Simone insisted on those occasions. "When you come in, leave that package of worry behind. Concentrate on us. We have a life, too."

Her dark eyes would flash at him, and her tiny body seemed electrically charged and ready to spark at the slightest provocation. He felt as if he walked on glass when they had these discussions.

Tony tried to discipline his feelings. She was young, and he understood that. But it was a struggle to submerge his doubts.

He realized just how troubled he was when he snapped at Mrs. Hazelitt, his longtime secretary, over a misplaced patient file. The motherly, grey-haired woman had actually taken a step back when he unexpectedly raised his voice.

Shaken, Tony quickly apologized.

"Forgive me, Mrs. H." He put his arms around her shoulders. "I'm just upset." He was indeed embarrassed that he had allowed himself to bring his personal problems into his professional life.

But it was a trifling argument over an extra set of keys that had caused a tear in the fabric of their marriage—some keys to the house, car, safe deposit boxes, offices, and the like.

"I want the keys in the front hall table drawer," Simone insisted.

"No, that's the first place a thief would look," Tony argued. "They'd be much better hidden in the kitchen in a canister, or in an empty coffee can."

He heard her continue, "Don't you know we don't even have any canisters?"

"That's because you never cook! You don't know what's in that kitchen!" Tony wanted to swallow the words right after he said them.

Simone's eyes flashed toward her husband like a hot flame torch. "And, dammit," she spat out the words, spaced and even, "I never will."

Tony ducked his head as the bunch of keys came sailing toward him.

Simone turned on her heels and strode from the room. Her footsteps sounded bold and defiant, a declaration of war.

Tony went to the living room and slumped into a chair. He was not accustomed to such behavior. How could Simone get so upset over his remark? Was the flaw in him or in her? He buried his head in his hands. He had always tried to be in control. As a physician, he had been taught to be that way.

Simone spoke to him from the living mom doorway. She was in her night clothes, looking, Tony thought, like a little girl. All she needed was a stuffed toy in her arms. He started toward her, but the chill in her voice stopped him.

"Tony, you needn't worry about me. I am accustomed to making decisions and judgments involving large sums of money belonging to my clients. I am very sure of myself and what I am doing."

Tony started to interrupt her, but she raised her hand to stop him.

"It seems to me you believe you must be in control and make all the decisions. Sorry, bro', that's not for me." She threw up both hands and shrugged her shoulders. "I'll be in the guest room tonight," she told him.

"Simone," Tony got to his feet, "what on earth are you talking about? This is only a set of keys." He held the keys in his hand.

"It's more than keys, Tony." This time her voice was pure ice, and she was gone.

Tony heard the guest room door slam down the corridor.

As she lay on the daybed in the guest room, Simone shivered under the thin blanket, sorry she had not remembered the lack of blankets available in the room before she impulsively opted to sleep apart from Tony. But she'd be damned if she'd go back to the linen closet for more covers and risk facing Tony again.

Chilled and angry, she got up and put on her robe, slipping her cold feet into her slippers. Tears stung under her eyelids as she kept hearing Tony's voice slamming at her about the keys. Didn't he know, realize, that she had never wanted to live in the South End? Why didn't he understand her better? Now if she was still married to Dayton, he would have agreed to anything she wanted.

Oh my God, she thought to herself, what am I doing thinking of Dayton? It's because of his phone call. How many years since their parents had separated the hapless pair—ten, at least. Why think about him tonight after her first real disagreement with her husband?

She wiped her eyes with a corner of the sheet and shook herself.

Simone, grow up! she told herself. *After all, at that time Dayton was a kid, and so was I. I can't have it both ways. If I'm going to be a married woman with a career, there are realities I have to face. But why did Tony think he was the only one who could be right? Make decisions? He always said he was proud of me and my accomplishments, but it seems that in the back of his mind, deep down, he really wants me more domestic and relegated to the kitchen. Was that really the problem?*

She finally dropped into a fitful sleep. She was roused restlessly each time she turned on the narrow, uncomfortable daybed, aware that she was not in her own bed with her husband's warm body beside her.

CHAPTER VI

Simone drove to her office on Monday, her mind in turmoil. A fleeting picture of her husband continually surfaced. She remembered his clean good looks, his warm smile, and the lyrical, almost poetic feeling she experienced when she was in his arms. Enough, enough, she thought to herself. She would deal with her personal problems when she could give them all of her attention. Usually she was so anxious to get to her office that she could hardly wait. She never knew what new challenge she would face, or what new idea would come across her desk. Sometimes, an idea seemed so "hot" it almost burned to be pursued.

This Monday morning, however, things were different. The "situation" between herself and Tony loomed large before her and cried for resolution. Her college roommate, Christine, had asked only a few questions when Simone had inquired whether she could stay with her for a few days.

"Anytime," her friend said. "You know you are welcome to stay as long as you need to. But I'm not happy with the way things are turning out between you and your husband," she added wisely.

Simone was grateful for the warm hug her former roommate gave her. Good friends were hard to find, and she would do the same for Chris. Chris knew that.

Simone's heels clicked a staccato beat across the floor as she went into her private office. The suite of rooms formed an office condominium that she was buying for her business. She barely spoke to her secretary. Her absent-minded "good morning" was returned to her in the same offhanded way by her secretary. Connie could read her boss' moods. Today might be one of those days. But Connie could deal with almost anything. Possessing a deep sense of loyalty to Simone, she also respected Simone's abilities in a world rarely opened to women. She was proud of Simone and would do anything for her. Connie would be patient. Whatever storm there was would pass.

Although isolated in her office, Simone could still hear sounds of activity. Connie's radio, set to a quiet, all-purpose music station, sent background melodies into the area. She heard the telephone ring, with Connie's voice responding to whatever query was posed. Outside her window, on Tremont Street, she was aware of vendors vying for limited parking space. Shouts from traffic officers, frustrated cabbies, and angry pedestrians pushed into her office. Her mind, troubled by inner chaos, could accept little more. She reached over and lowered the blinds. Perhaps that would diminish some of the disorder she was experiencing.

Disappointment was not something she handled well. Always, before, it seemed that things in her life had a way of working in her favor. Could it be that she had been spoiled to expect good fortune to be ever at her side? The picture of Tony, confused and bewildered with the keys in his hands, rose like a gorge in her throat. It buzzed in the recesses of her mind like a nagging mosquito. The persistent, abiding truth was that life would go on despite the fact that she and Tony were at odds.

She turned her attention to her desk. At the alumni dance she had been introduced to a military officer from one of the nearby bases. Hancomb Mercer, a brigadier general, planned to retire soon. His intent was to make a career change and to work out his retirement future, and he had been introduced to Simone as the person to help him. Noting on her calendar that he was due in at eleven that morning, she rang for Connie.

"Look, Connie, do you remember that file on acquisitions I asked you to set aside for me?"

"Do you want it now?" The secretary turned to leave the office. "It's right on my desk."

"Oh, no, not at the moment. General Mercer will be here this morning, and I'd like to look it over before he comes in."

Connie breathed with relief. Her employer was back in stride. The agitation she had noticed early that morning had been replaced by competence and reassurance.

"And, Connie, remember that article in the *Wall Street Journal* I asked you to save? I know that General Mercer was stationed in West Germany. I'd like to get his views on the changing market there. With the fall of the Berlin Wall and the new European market, it may be a place to invest. I plan to do some research on the possibilities, especially the Eastern Bloc countries.

"And...current research recommends investing in Africa. Many American companies—IBM, Coca-Cola, Microsoft are extending in the direction."

So Simone started her day. She pushed her marital problem into the back corner of her mind. Like other career women before her, she would pull it forward and deal with it later, and in its time.

The next morning in his office, after a sleepless night, Tony wrestled with his problem. On his desk, Mrs. Hazelitt had placed the folders of the patients he would see that day. He picked up the first one the Sheltons, each thirty-seven years old. They had gone through $35,000 in the past fourteen years in an attempt to have a baby.

Tony stared at the folder, trying to focus on his plan for the couple. The frustration, anger, and even impotence that he felt from the previous evening's episode was maddening and kept crowding into his mind. He was as angry with himself as with Simone. How could he have been so wrong about his wife? Could his judgment of human behavior have been that far off? Was it only the sex between them that held them together? What was the problem?

He thought of all the years of difficult days and nights struggling through college on hard-earned scholarships, of doing distasteful jobs from busboy to morgue attendant to get through medical school, of being constantly reminded, "It's not for your kind, you should be taking a trade," of being shunned because he was trying to "make it." He recalled the stinging feelings of rage he had had to swallow when the chief of surgery goaded him when he was completing a total hysterectomy on a patient under his supervision. "No, doctor," the white man had said sarcastically, "you are doing this all wrong! Can't you see that vessel you are about to cut?" Tony remembered how difficult it had been that day not to retaliate, since he knew he was following the correct procedure. But he was too close to completion of his residency to be "washed out" because he couldn't hold his tongue. He knew how easily that could happen. It had been even more difficult to be civil when the chief spoke to him in the doctors' lounge after the humiliating experience.

"Housner, you've a great pair of surgical hands. I liked your technique and, I must say, you don't fold under pressure." Tony's face flushed with the memory as he relived the anger he had felt.

"Oh, Simone," he murmured to himself. He had felt so complete when she had come into his life. He had thought that he knew her, that she wanted the same things he did—to build a loving life together, full of enjoyment. A life with creature comforts and security all the things he had dreamed of having during each one of those "scut bucket" hours of study and work. He knew that he loved Simone but was it only a physical, sexual attraction? Could he—should he believe that something was there worth fighting for and working toward? Could he live with her mercurial, volatile personality?

Sighing, he opened the Sheltons' folder. He could hear footsteps outside his office door. That would be Mrs. Hazelitt, with a cup of coffee for him. His day's work was about to begin, and his personal problems would have to be pushed aside.

As he reviewed the folder, he could visualize Mrs. Shelton, a moderately obese blond woman who was a fifth grade teacher. She had suffered prior damage to her fallopian tubes and, because of this, normal pregnancy could not occur. Repeated surgical repairs had not been beneficial. Jonathan Shelton, her husband, was starting his first elected term as a member of the Massachusetts House of Representatives. They lived in a small farming community two hours' drive from Boston, near the Vermont state line. They desperately wanted a child, and their physician had referred them to Pioneer Women's Hospital and Dr Anton Housner.

Tony smiled to himself as he remembered the looks of incredulity on their faces the first time they entered his office and saw the African-American doctor sitting behind the desk.

"Are you...you're Dr. Anton Housner?" the husband stuttered, unbelievingly.

"Yes, indeed I am," Tony said, extending his hand to Mr. Shelton. He offered Mrs. Shelton a comfortable chair and waved toward the wall. "That's what it says on all those papers." A half-dozen framed diplomas and certificates were arranged on his office wall.

The Sheltons had now been consulting Tony for almost a year. He had prescribed drugs to stimulate Mrs. Shelton's ovaries to produce eggs. Because the decision had been made to attempt in vitro fertilization to impregnate her, eggs had been surgically retrieved from Mrs. Shelton and then mixed with her husband's sperm in a Petri dish in the laboratory. The technique had been successful, and the eggs fertilized. Then, in another surgical procedure, Mrs. Shelton's damaged fallopian tubes had been bypassed and the fertile egg implanted into her uterus. There had been several "no-takes," but then nine months ago, to everyone's delight, there had been a successful implantation. Now the happy couple was expecting their first child.

When they came through the door, Tony's first thought was, *Well, it's nice to be a part of someone's happiness.* He could see it on their bright, eager faces.

"Dr Housner," the husband began to speak, "how can we tell you how happy we are?" His face flushed a bright red as he tried to keep his emotions under control. "You can't know what you have given us."

"Well," Tony beamed, "let's hope for a beautiful, healthy baby which I, for one, believe you're going to have."

Mrs. Shelton spoke up, "The way this baby is kicking, I know it's going to be healthy. And…Dr. Housner, we want you to know if it's a boy, it will be Jonathan Anton Shelton, and if it's a girl, Joanna Antonia Shelton."

"I'm pleased and flattered, Mrs. Shelton. Now let's get you into the examining room and check things out. You're feeling well?" he questioned.

"Couldn't be better," she smiled at the man who had made her dream a reality.

When he was growing up, Tony's mother had often said, "Helping others, involving yourself in the lives of others, gives greater rewards than you can imagine." She had always been a helping hand in their tightly knit black community. When Tony and his brother Bart came home from school, there might be a note on the refrigerator door: "Over at the Andersons'—dinner in the oven," or "David's mother taken to hospital; back soon."

Tony found satisfaction in his practice. He once told Simone, "It's like you're a part of another person's family when you're involved in a caring profession like medicine. The rush you get when you deliver a healthy baby to brand-new parents is unbelievable. Everyone in the delivery room has a wide grin on his or her face. And it doesn't matter whether it's your first delivery that day or your tenth. It's always a thrill."

"I guess so, Tony," Simone said. "I do know some satisfaction, too, when one of my clients is pleased with a successfully managed portfolio."

Tony agreed. "It's because you like what you do, and you do it well. I'm not making comparisons in our work, hon. I just wanted to share a little of mine with you. And you know I'm always anxious to know about your work."

But she made only brief references to her own work, almost as if she were afraid of any criticisms her husband might make.

Simone, the middle child in her family, had an older sibling, Cleo, who was extremely attractive. Not only did Cleo have a striking appearance, but she was a compliant, pleasant child. Simone's parents often chided their younger daughter with, "Why aren't you more like your sister?"

"Boy, did that make me mad," Simone told her roommate, Christine Langley.

The two had been watching a television story that portrayed the life of a troubled family.

Christine, legs doubled up under her as she sat on the couch, leaned toward the coffee table to pick up a snack. "Why did it make you mad?"

"It made me mad because I didn't think there was anything wrong with me. I was just me," Simone answered. She went on, "And to make matters worse, when I was about three, my baby brother was born. I wanted to kill him!"

"Simone, you must have been a handful for your folks."

"I was. I was always into something. I think I was uncertain of my place in the family and was always calling attention to myself to make sure they knew they had me there."

She shook her head and laughed, "I'll never forget the day my brother Dana was in the baby carriage, crying his head off. I tried to stop his crying and, as I remember it, I was swinging the carriage back and forth, back and forth, swinging it so hard that the baby almost fell out onto the floor My mother came out. 'What are you doing?' she asked. I told her, 'Trying to make him stop crying.' "

Christine laughed. "It's a wonder your mother didn't give you a good spanking. Mine would have."

"You know, Chris," Simone told her, "in her place I would have, too, but I think my poor mother knew what I needed. I remember well her talking to my father, saying, 'Henry, that child needs more attention. Can you give it to her?'"

"And did he?" Chris wanted to know.

Simone puffed out her cheeks and let out a big sigh.

"Honey, I'm more my father's son than my brother is. Daddy took me everywhere. He taught me tennis. I ran the high hurdles in high school because he was a track star in college. I ran the 100 meters. I was determined to please him, and I did everything I could. People used to say, 'Here comes Henry Harper and his spittin' image, Simone.' Tennis matches, track meets, driving from city to city school to school—I've always loved being with him."

"You told me your dad was a high school principal in Richmond, right?" Christine asked.

"He is retired now, but he loves that school. Integrated now, but he moved into that situation with ease."

"You really love him, huh, Simone?"

"I do. I remember one time, my senior year in high school, I was trying out for the state championship in the high hurdles. I desperately wanted to make the team. I lost, and I was so upset—didn't see how I could face Dad. He found me out behind the bleachers, throwing up. I was so sick! He helped me dean up, then pushed me out to face my competition and my defeat. 'Look, Simone,' he said, 'losing means learning. Look at what made you lose, think about what you did wrong. Analyze your errors and put them where they belong—in your bag of I-won't-do-that-again memories.' Chris, I think my competitive nature came from my father. When I think about him, I feel all warm and my insides curl with delight. I always wanted to be like him."

Christine was quiet and thoughtful as she looked at Simone. Finally she spoke. "Simone, your relationship with your husband shouldn't be a competitive one. Have you tried to make it one?"

Christine saw quick anger flood her roommate's face. She threw up her hands in mock defense. "Just asking," she said.

"No, I'm not competing with Tony. It's just that I want him to recognize my value, that's all," Simone said.

Simone had been staying at Chris' apartment for a few days. "We need some time away from each other so we can sort things out," she told Tony.

"I don't," Tony said. "You're my wife. I love you, and I believe that if we talk out our differences together, things will be just fine," he reminded her in a firm voice.

He was determined to do just that. A weekend away from Boston might do it. Skiing in Vermont, perhaps.

In his senior year of pre-med, he had spent a winter semester at McGill University in Montreal. Introduced to skiing, he learned to love the sport. To his great delight, Simone was an accomplished skier. When he called her and asked her about a weekend trip, she agreed. He told her he would have Mrs. Hazelitt make all the reservations.

When Tony awakened that Friday morning, his mind seemed to be dancing in delight in anticipation of a new beginning. But he was almost afraid to move, afraid of disturbing the beautiful thought of being with Simone.

"Let it be perfect," he prayed. "Please, let it be perfect for us."

He'd have to get moving. It was Friday, and there would be patients to see. Mrs. Shelton, for one, would be coming in for her first checkup after delivery. He knew she'd be bringing pictures of Jonathan Anton Shelton. He smiled as he stepped into the shower. Babies do bring love. Maybe that's what Simone needed. But first things first. He'd have to get her back. Try to remove whatever the barrier was that lay between them.

CHAPTER VII

Simone was waiting for Tony in Chris' apartment lobby. When she saw his car swing into the driveway, she motioned to him to stay in the car. She hurried over with her weekend bag, which she threw into the backseat.

"Hi," she smiled at Tony. "Glad the snow stopped."

Tony answered with enthusiasm. "Me too. I was worried we might be driving toward a snowstorm, but the weatherman says it's all gone out to sea. Should be a good weekend. Simone, you look great!"

"Thanks, Tony, you don't look so bad yourself."

Tony grinned and put the car in gear. "Ski country, here come the Housners," he whooped. "Here's to us, my love."

Boston was beautiful that Friday evening. The usually grimy old streets had been covered by a soft coverlet of newly fallen snow. The sky was dear and the moon bright. Sparkles of light reflected from the snow-covered buildings, the trees, and the cars that sped through the city.

Tony was almost beside himself with joy. He had his wife with him, where she belonged. When Simone, sensing his mood, smiled at him, his heart did an unexpected somersault.

What was it about this tiny slip of a girl that intrigued him so? He'd known many attractive women in his life, but Simone? Part of it was the high excitement that seized him when she was near him. There was her strong will, her directness, her strength of character. She saw things as they really were. No pretense. And…her beauty. Her perfectly molded chin, the challenge of her lovely eyes, framed by lashes so thick they seemed like black paint smudges. Tonight, in the flashing lights from passing cars, she looked exceptionally desirable. She was wearing a body-hugging ski suit of turquoise nylon with soft peach trim on the collar and cuffs. Her ski pants were black, with a peach and turquoise stripe along the pant legs. She wore grey nylon and split suede leather hiking boots with turquoise inner linings and lacings. Because the car was warm, she had thrown back her hood and unzipped her jacket to reveal a peach-colored, cotton turtleneck shirt. Tony grasped the steering wheel firmly and reminded himself that he'd have to keep his mind on his driving. Was she ever lovely!

Simone inserted a cassette into the car's tape deck, and soft sounds of subtle jazz filled the cat

"That's real nice, Sim. What is it? Who's singing?" Tony asked as he checked his rearview mirror for the traffic behind him.

"It's a guy from England. Says he has listened to famous black artists from the States since he was a kid. Now he's singing just like they did."

"White people always have had a way of copying our music," Tony said. "He does sound just like a brother."

"I know," Simone agreed. "He really does."

They listened for awhile. Simone looked at her husband.

"Tony?"

"Yes, Sim?"

"Are you angry with me for the way I left?" Her voice was very quiet.

"Well, Simone," he peered through the darkened night, "I really don't know if angry is the right word."

"What is it, then?" Simone turned in her seat to look at him.

"Simone, I just don't see how a discussion over where to put a set of keys could have caused the situation like the one we're in now. I mean...I'm not so much angry as I am disappointed and hurt. I thought we loved each other and that we wanted the same things. I guess the right words are pain and disappointment. That's what I felt."

"Disappointment was what I felt, too, Tony. It seems to me that you feel you're always right. It wasn't really the keys themselves, but what they stood for in your mind. Just as you made the decision to buy the brownstone when you knew I wanted to live in the suburbs. You didn't consider my wants. You had made the decision, and that was that. Then, when you threw in that bit about my not being in the kitchen...well," her voice trailed off.

"Oh, honey," Tony said softly, "I know you have ideas and opinions. That's one of the traits I admire in you—your independence and your strong self-concept. I wouldn't have you any other way. And you are wrong if you think I only want you in the kitchen."

He reached over and patted her knee.

"Let's not mention keys for the rest of the weekend, okay?"

"Okay, Tony." She'd leave it for now, she thought.

They left the city lights of Boston behind them and sped toward the hills of New Hampshire. They drove in comfortable silence, listening to the tapes that Simone had brought, and headed across the Connecticut River at White River Junction.

"Would you like to stop for coffee when we get to White River Junction?" Tony suggested. "Maybe we could get a sandwich. It might be too late for dinner when we reach the lodge."

"Sounds like a good idea to me. How much longer before we get there?" Simone questioned.

"I believe we have a couple more hours of driving. Its not that far in miles, but we're going up into the mountains, and that makes it much slower."

Noticing a small restaurant called Pete's Highway Pantry just after they left the town's center, they decided to stop, drove into a circular driveway, and parked. As they stepped out of the car, the crisp, cold Vermont air took their breath away. The snow crunched beneath their boots as they ran into the clean and brightly lit building. A massive stone fireplace at the far end of the room drew them like a magnet and welcomed them with a roaring fire.

A waitress came over to them and said, "If you'd like, we can pull a table right up close to the fire for you."

"Would you?" Tony asked. "That would be so nice."

He helped the young waitress arrange a table and chairs, then helped Simone take off her jacket.

"Would you like a cup of vegetable soup or onion soup to start?" the waitress asked. "And the special for tonight is chicken pot pie."

Simone nodded to the waitress.

"The vegetable soup sounds good, and the chicken pie, too. Could I have a small green salad with oil and vinegar?"

"Yes, ma'am, and you, sir?" she looked at Tony.

"I'll have the same, thanks."

Tony had not really wanted to delay their arrival at the lodge. He had thought a sandwich would suffice, but now it appeared it would be even longer before he would have Simone in his arms again. What they had shared was so special, he wanted to get back to the happiness they had had before the misunderstanding. He *had* to win his wife back. Patience and loving care, that's what he would show her.

It turned out to be quite a pleasant meal. First they were served a hearty vegetable soup rich with beef broth, followed by flaky-topped chicken pie in individual casseroles. Good portions of chicken in a filling not too thick or heavy—just perfect to hold all the ingredients together.

Simone ate her salad first.

"I've always liked to eat one thing at a time," she told Tony. "My parents could never break me of that habit. I would just go at one thing, one vegetable or my salad, eat that, and move on to the next item. Isn't that weird?" she asked him. "Guess I'm one-minded."

"You're entitled," Tony said. "Enjoy your meal, Sim. I want everything perfect for you this weekend."

"I know," she said as she bent her head forward over her plate.

What's he going to say, she wondered to herself, when he finds out what I've done? She remembered Mrs. Hazelitt's hesitation when she had asked the secretary to book a single room for her at the lodge.

"You want me to do what?" the woman's astonishment was very clear over the telephone.

"I know you're making the reservations for the weekend, Mrs. Hazelitt, but I would prefer a room of my own."

Mrs. Hazelitt's voice came back, measured and dry.

"I don't mean to get into your business, my dear, but you do know that Dr Housner is planning this weekend as a second honeymoon? I've never seen him so excited. A single room..." her voice trailed off.

"This weekend is very important to me, too," Simone pushed on. "It will make or break our marriage. Tony has got to realize that I'm not a weak, flighty female over whom he can have total control."

Mrs. Hazelitt pressed her case. "I'll do as you ask, but I'm going to tell you something. My little bit of advice. And I'll not interfere any more. There are only a few good men of color out there, and..." Simone heard the woman take a deep breath before she continued, "you have lucked up on a wonderful man—one of the best, who loves you deeply. You know the old saying, 'Don' worry about dat mule goin' blin' jump in de wagon and pic' up de lines.' It's one of the things my grandmother used to say."

"Yes, I know"

"You know what the saying means—take what you have and keep going forward. Nothing is perfect, you know."

That conversation ran around in Simone's mind. What will Tony say what will he do when he finds out what I've done? she asked herself.

She glanced at him as he ate. This was the man she loved, she knew that. However, she had always tried to mask her feelings of insecurity perhaps brought on by being the middle sibling by projecting a facade of independence.

She had always tried to be tough, because she thought she had to be. Anyone with an older, beautiful sister and a younger brother had to show toughness and resilience, or not be noticed. So she became independent and strong—at least it seemed that way to others. Even Tony had said tonight that he admired her "strong self-concept." Underneath was a little girl searching for steadfast love. Did Tony see that? Could he have enough patience to endure? To accept her faults?

She cleared her throat.

Tony looked up.

"Tony, I don't want you to be mad with me."

"Why should I be mad? We're starting over, aren't we? Putting the past behind us."

He reached for her hand.

"It's going to be wonderful, you'll see."

It was now or never. Simone lost no time; the words tumbled out of her mouth.

"I asked Mrs. H to book a single room for me at the lodge."

Simone saw Tony's eyes narrow in bewilderment and disbelief as her words penetrated into his brain. Quickly she pulled her hand from his grasp.

In a low, steady voice filled with anger, he growled, "You did what?"

"Tony!' Simone drew a deep breath, "I said I'd spend the weekend with you skiing. I didn't say I'd sleep with you."

"I don't believe this!" He slammed his fist on the table. "I get one of my few weekends off, run all over the hospital checking my patients, get Dr. Engles to cover for me..."

He scrutinized his wife's face as if to be certain of who this woman really was, then continued his tirade.

"Here we are, with reservations at one of the most expensive ski resorts in the Northeast, we've driven almost two hundred miles, and you mean to tell me that you, my lawful wife, can't stand to spend two nights in bed with me?"

"Tony, I...," Simone tried to speak.

She had never seen Tony so angry. And she was almost frightened at the pain she saw in his face. It seemed to be breaking apart, as if she had struck him a physical blow.

"Don't 'Tony, I' me!" he exploded. "Sim, I think you've gone too far. You've had me dancing on a gibbet like a crazy man for too long now. I've had it."

Simone's mouth was dry from fear.

She realized she had wounded her husband immeasurably. She could feel his pain.

Could she make him understand? She tried again.

"Tony, I came with you this weekend because I do want a reconciliation. I want to save our marriage—but I don't want it to be merely a sexual thing. I need to know that you see me as a partner. Not just someone to have good sex with, but a real partner a contributing partner in our life together." She watched her husband's face for his reaction, then pursued her point. "Like your buying the brownstone without any input from me."

"Oh, God, not that again!" Tony interrupted. "You're beating a dead horse. I already agreed that I was wrong when I did that, but don't you see, I was acting in what I thought were our best interests."

His forehead was a mass of frowns as he peered with narrowed eyes at Simone.

"We've got to try to get past that, girl, if we're going to make a new start!"

"Don't you see?" she insisted. "If we jump into bed together, that's not a new start. We will still have our real differences and problems to sort out."

"You say we have problems! The only problem is your pigheaded, childish stubbornness! Why don't you grow up! By rights," he muttered as he counted out money for their meals, "by all that makes any sense, I should turn this car around and go back to Boston."

Simone got up quickly from the table and shrugged into her ski jacket. As they hurried out of the restaurant, her short legs quickened to keep pace with her angry husband's long stride.

Outside, the sky was black velvet and the stars shone like elegant diamond studs in the ebony heavens—but Simone could not enjoy or savor the beauty of her surroundings. She took a deep breath as she got into the car. Tony was silent, his face dark with anger. He had turned up the collar of his wool parka, and the gesture created a barrier between them. It was as if he did not even want to see Simone. She shivered from the isolation as well as from the cold. Did her husband know that she really did care what about happened to them?

Tony felt small and diminished, and he wanted to withdraw into himself for comfort and validation of his own self-worth. Simone had hurt him grievously. He did not see how he could stand much more of her crazy behavior. He didn't understand her. They drove for the next hour in silence.

Simone stared out into the dark night. Tears welled in her eyes, but she would not let them fall.

"Never, never show weakness," her Dad used to say. "Stay strong and pull yourself together, even if it kills you."

She reached forward and placed another cassette in the tape deck. Count Basie's jazz filled the car and settled into the spaces of their silence. The car moved forward in the dark night, each occupant aware of the uncertain future that lay before them. Somehow they arrived at their destination, an Austrian-type lodge deep in the northern mountains of Vermont. They had not spoken since leaving the restaurant.

Simone picked up her overnight bag, but Tony wrestled it out of her hand.

"I have it," he said brusquely as they followed the Tyrolean-costumed bellhop to their rooms.

Her room number was 333, located right next to his. They went into her room first. Simone had money in her hand for a tip for the porter, but Tony placed himself between her and the man and proceeded to give him a sizable amount of money. Simone saw several bills exchange hands.

Each made covert glances at the inviting king-size bed in the room. Its presence encouraged thoughts of passion and love. Each knew what the other was thinking—not tonight, sadly.

Simone walked with Tony to the door. Unexpectedly he bent down to kiss her cheek and murmured, "Be sure to lock the door. *I'm* not promising to stay in my room. You could have a guest." As if he couldn't trust himself, he hurried out. "See you at breakfast." He was gone.

Simone turned the lock in the door and placed the security chain in position. She threw herself on the bed, and the unshed tears flooded her eyes. Tension and anxiety overcame her. She realized that every fiber of her body wanted to be with her husband. What was she doing alone in a strange room? She wanted Tony. She wanted to let herself be loved, and she wanted to love Tony—to run her fingers along his cheekbones, caress his forehead, steal his breath from his mouth with soft kisses. She wanted to feel his strong, loving hands as they explored her body—as they eased the ache in her breasts. She wanted to curl her thighs around his slender, powerful legs and soar with him to dizzy heights of ecstasy.

Everything was wrong. She felt wretched. She got up and prepared herself for bed, crying so hard that she could hardly see what she was doing.

At last under the blankets, she reached to put out the table lamp. In the dark, she felt lonely and abandoned. She cried herself to sleep.

Angry and disappointed, Tony stared out of the window into the cold Vermont night. What could he have done to Simone to make her behave this way?

At times like this he wished he had taken up smoking. People who smoked seemed to find instant peace as they puffed and exhaled, as if blowing all their troubles away. But smoking had never appealed to him; it was dirty, expensive, and it killed. As a physician, he had seen countless lives cut short by King Nicotine, a dreadful and addictive drug. But tonight, as he sat distressed by the turn of events the night had brought, he needed a pacifier of some sort. Perhaps he'd call room service and have something sent up. But it wasn't food he needed…it was his wife.

He prepared for bed in the darkened room, and as he climbed under the sheets, he continued to think about his dilemma.

Could it be that Simone had a physical problem that had escaped his notice? She was a hard worker and had not let up on meeting her clients' deadlines, he knew. Could she be hiding something from him? Should he check with her gynecologist, Dr. Savigen? He tried to remember when

Simone had had her last checkup. There had to be some reason for her volatile behavior.

As he lay thinking, he thought about the last time he and his wife had spent together talking. They had returned one evening after attending a concert at Symphony Hall. The Boston Symphony had been brilliant, as usual, and the guest soloist was a young, exciting, talented trumpeter from New Orleans. As a frustrated would-be trumpet player, Tony had enjoyed the evening's performance. He felt expansive and talkative as he and Simone went over the evening's activities together

"What I wouldn't have given to be able to play like that young man tonight," he told her as he took off his tuxedo jacket.

"What stopped you?" Simone inquired.

"My father died, and there was no more money for trumpet lessons, Boy Scouts, camp, any of those things."

"Poor baby," Simone crooned to Tony as she removed her shoes and prepared to undress. She went over to Tony, turning her back to him so he could unzip her dress.

"Oh, I don't know. My father's death made a really big hole in our lives, that I do know. But my mother, God bless her, tried her best to fill in the gaps. Things like music lessons, camp, and vacations you could do without. Oh, you'd miss them for a while, but the most important thing was to have food and a roof over your head. Those things we had, and I'll tell you something else, Sim…"

"What?" Simone stepped out of her dress.

"I grew up overnight. I was a twelve-year-old boy one day, and the next day I was a twelve-year-old man."

"How did your mother keep you in school?" Simone wanted to know. "She had to work, didn't she?"

"One of her sisters lived down the street, so we—my mother and I would go to my aunt's house after school until my mother picked us up. Soon I was in junior high school, and mother felt we could be on our own to get home to do our homework and the chores she had assigned to us."

"So that's how you got to be so good with housework, my love," Simone chuckled as she shrugged into her bathrobe.

"Damn straight!" Tony responded. "My mother was strict, but very loving. She's always been that way. She could rip you up one side and down the other for some mistake you made, but right after that she'd be shoving a piece of chocolate cake or apple pie in your face, saying, 'You love me?' No matter how severe the punishment, you'd say, 'Yes, Momma,' because really you did. And you knew she loved you and wanted only the best."

Simone disappeared into the bathroom, and when she came out, Tony lay in bed, patting the other side as an invitation to his wife.

When she settled in, Tony turned toward her.

"Did I ever tell you about Momma and the guidance counselor at school?"

"I don't think so, Tony. What happened?"

Simone placed her head on her husband's shoulder and he pulled the comforter over them.

"Well, it was time to decide which courses to take in high school. You know, after my father died so suddenly, I wondered, could medicine have saved him? And I told my mother the day of my dad's funeral that I wanted to study medicine, to help people, so no more fathers would die and leave their families."

"You had high ideals even then, Tony."

"I know, but when I saw my mother standing in the kitchen that day, stuffing a face cloth in her mouth to keep from screaming out her grief, I guess I thought I had to say something."

"What did she say to you?"

"She said, 'I will do all that I can to help you, son, and if you get the grades you need and study hard, with God's help you will be a doctor some day!' "

"So where does the guidance counselor come in?"

"When the time came to select my high school courses, I told the counselor that I wanted to take the college courses to study to be a doctor. He almost laughed in my face. He told me that I should take a trade course so that I could go into the arsenal and learn to make guns. My father had worked there as a crane operator, so I guess he thought I'd want to follow my dad in the gun shop. He said, 'You know your mother needs the money, and if you take a trade, learn to operate a machine, you can be making good money in no time.' "

"So you went home and told your mother?"

"She hit the ceiling! You know my mother is a tall woman, and the counselor was a small man, so when my mother strode into his office he turned positively green. As I remember it, he had white hair and, shaking behind his desk, he looked like one of the seven dwarfs."

"What did your mother tell him?"

Tony rubbed his hand along Simone's shoulder as he drew her closer to him. "Told that little old white man that he was to make *no* decisions regarding her son's future. That only she had the right to do that. She birthed me, and she would decide what was best for her child. Hadn't he heard of equal opportunity? And when he nodded his head, scared to death of Momma, she said that was *all* she wanted for her sons: equal opportunity. And if *he* knew what was in his best interests, he'd better see that her children got it."

"That man had never seen anyone like your mother, Tony, I'll bet!"

"This was true and you know, Simone, my mother never let up on me. Anytime I got discouraged, she'd remind me of that time. 'Want to be in a machine shop, making guns?' she'd ask. And that teacher, Mr. Timora, died just before I graduated from medical school. Momma said she wanted to go over to his grave and wave my sheepskin. 'See, I told you all my child needed was a chance!' she said she wanted to say."

"Tony, you must be proud of your mom."

"I am—and I'm proud of you, too, Simone. Like Momma, you have determination. That's one of the things that attracted me to you, young lady."

"Ummm, anything else?" Simone laughed.

"You bet, my love," Tony said as he gathered her into his arms. They both giggled as they nestled under the covers like two kids at play. Their lovemaking was sweet and satisfying to each of them.

Tony sighed at his memory of that night. He had anticipated a reprise of that night, tonight—but he couldn't make Simone share his bed, nor would he want to force her. He loved her too much for that. He'd have to find out the problem and do his best to correct it.

There had to be a way.

CHAPTER VIII

"Dr. Housner?"

The voice on the telephone sounded strange in Tony's ear. He had awakened on the first ring, a habit formed by a doctor's many midnight calls. "Yes?" he grunted as he struggled to orient himself. Ah, yes, he was in Vermont, he remembered.

"Dr. Housner, this is Mrs. Hazelitt. I'm sorry to disturb you, but there's a problem at the hospital lab."

"A problem? What kind of problem? What's happened, Mrs. Hazelitt?"

"A break-in of some sort. The police think that someone was looking for drugs or money and, well, they just about trashed the place. The hospital director would like you to get back here and..."

"What time is it now?" Tony sat up in bed, struggling to dear sleep from his mind.

"It's four-thirty. Can you get back today? Doctor, I'm so sorry this happened."

"That's all right, Mrs. Hazelitt. I'll try to get a flight out of Burlington."

Simone arrived in the dining room around eight the next morning. It had been a bad night for her; her sleep had been restless. She had dreamed about her father and Tony. They were playing tennis with such hostility that she thought they were going to kill each other. She woke up wringing wet with perspiration, her nightgown clinging like a cold shroud.

She felt better after a hot shower. She put on a pair of camel-colored wool slacks and a soft gold cashmere sweater. She brushed her hair until it fairly crackled and made up her facewith just enough sheen to look healthy and glowing.

Oh, Tony, she thought, *please see me for what I am and love me as a real woman.* Not someone you can control and manage like a little girl.

The dining room was bright and sunny. Windows along the outer wall had skylights over them that flooded the room with sunshine. Flowers were everywhere—on the tables, along the windowsills, and on the floor surrounding a long buffet table filled with food. One of the waitresses who was dressed in an Austrian costume, her blonde hair knotted in heavy braids, welcomed Simone to a table.

"Coffee, madam?"

"Oh, yes, please. It smells so good."

Where was Tony anyway? Somehow Simone felt anxious to get the day started. Would they get off on the right foot today?

As she sipped the hot coffee, her anxiety lessened. She'd have to get her husband to understand her need to be independent. She had never thought that he'd view it as being stubborn, obstinate, and childish.

"For breakfast there is the buffet table or, if you wish, you may order from the menu," the waitress told Simone.

"I am expecting Dr. Housner to join me for breakfast," Simone told the waitress as she accepted the menu. "I'll wait for him."

Simone did not notice Tony at the dining room entrance. He spoke to the maitre d', gave the man an envelope, and pointed to Simone. Then he left.

The maitre d' took the envelope to Simone.

"Mrs. Housner, Dr Housner asked me to give you this."

"Oh," Simone asked, "where is he?"

"He's left, I believe," the man told her

Confused, Simone opened the envelope. Car keys and several ski lift tickets fell out onto the table, along with a note.

"Dearest Simone," she read. "I have to return to Boston. Have taken a taxi to Burlington to catch an early flight. Mrs. H. called—there was a problem at the lab. Stay and enjoy the snow. Here are tickets to the ski lift and keys to my BMW. Be careful driving back. All the best plans—eh? All my love, Tony."

Bone tired, Simone let herself into the Brookline apartment. Christine, her roommate, was in the bathroom. She came out with a towel around her head when she heard Simone come in.

"Girl, what are you doing here? You're supposed to be in Vermont."

Simone fell onto the sofa and flung her arms wide in a gesture of fatigue.

"Just drove 212 miles from Vermont. I'm bushed."

"Where's Tony? What happened?" Chris asked.

"What happened, if anything, is that everything is worse," Simone groaned. "To tell you the truth, Chris, I really think my marriage to Tony has drawn its last breath—all we need to do now is pronounce it dead!"

"Come on, don't say that. Tell me what happened," Christine said.

Simone could see the worried concern in Chris' face.

"We had sort of a fight…well, I…" She didn't want to reveal to her roommate that she had opted for a single room; in review, it did seem silly. Slowly she continued, "Tony was called back in the middle of the night. Some problem at his lab—he flew back, and I drove the car back from Vermont."

"Now what?" Christine asked.

"I'll let him know I made it back. Probably call him later. Right now I want to shower and get a little rest. And," she added wryly, "do a little thinking."

Later that evening, Simone called her husband. She reached his answering service and left a message saying that she had returned. She asked him to call her on Sunday—and she told him she hoped there was not too much trouble at the lab.

Early Sunday morning, Tony called.

"Simone, I'm glad you made it back all right. Any trouble with the car?"

"No," she answered, surprised at the lack of animosity in her husband's voice. It was as if there had been no strain between them. "The car drove beautifully. Tony, what happened at your lab? I was worried."

"Well, thanks. There was a break-in. Desks and files were broken into, papers and charts all over the place. But my frozen embryos were not disturbed. I have several implantations scheduled for the next few months, and I was really worried about them."

"Probably someone looking for drugs or money," Simone offered.

"The police think so. And they think that because the lab is in an isolated part of the hospital complex, whoever it was figured they'd have easy access. The police are doing the usual fingerprints, investigating, questioning everybody. The usual. Listen, Simone I'm still free until Monday morning. Do you feel up to dinner tonight? I've got to pick up the car..."

"Tony, dinner would be fine, if we can do it early. About six?"

"See you at six. Don't forget, Simone, we *will* have a new start."

"Okay, Tony." Simone was not at all certain, and a twinge of guilt flickered around the edges of her mind. Tony did not know about her impending trip to the West Coast. She had not been able to tell him that she'd be out of the city for the next few days. She would do it tonight. She dreaded his reaction.

Sunday was one of those late winter days when the sun's rays warm the earth with a promise of spring. Most of the snow had melted, and the black pavement glistened like a ribbon of wet satin as Tony drove them to Scituate.

The Massachusetts harbor town had several restaurants just inside the harbor, and Tony had chosen Simone's favorite. It had exposed beams and huge windows that gave a beautiful view of the active harbor. Boats, with their red and green night lights, meandered along quietly. The tables were wood, with a high gloss, and the cushioned captain's chairs made diners feel special. Paintings of old ships, as well as figureheads, whaling gear, and scrimshaw, hung on the walls of the room, all in keeping with the nautical atmosphere.

Simone smiled when she sat in the comfortable chair. Despite everything, she did feel content when she was with her husband. He had a natural talent for making her feel that way. She only wanted him to understand her and appreciate her more. He always seemed happiest when he was in charge, as if he alone could make decisions. Why was he like that, she wondered, and why did she rail at authority when she enjoyed being cared for?

The food was good. They both had zucchini and rice soup, followed by a salad of glazed beets and fresh leeks with vinaigrette dressing. Tony ordered flank steak with garlic, ginger, and soy sauce, while Simone had stuffed lobster with crabmeat dressing. For dessert they were served a slice of chocolate cake with a white chocolate sauce and black coffee.

Tony ordered a small brandy for each of them. They both knew it was time to talk. Tony leaned back in his chair and looked at his wife.

"Simone, do you realize how much I love you? And do you know how hurt I felt Friday night when you threw that bomb at me?"

"Tony, I didn't mean to hurt you, but you can infuriate me so, trying to direct my life—every move I make, every thought I have. And I won't let my independence be taken from me! I've struggled all my life to be an individual, separate but equal, and..."

"Why, then, Simone, did you marry me?" Tony questioned, his face taut with strain.

"Because..." her voice was low as she rubbed her fingers distractedly around the top of her brandy glass, "because I love you."

"Well, when are you coming home, back where you belong?"

"I can't," she said. "I'm leaving tomorrow for San Francisco. I'll be there for a few days. I'm giving a seminar on financial planning."

Simone's announcement stopped Tony's hand in mid-air as he raised his brandy glass to his lips. When he replaced his drink on the table, the cold anger in his voice seemed to freeze the air in the room.

"Simone," he said slowly, his face a mask of stone, the usual warmth in his eyes an impassive stare that seemed to push Simone further back in her large chair as though for protection. His tone was one of painful reproach.

"Now," he continued, "now I realize that you don't love me. Not at all, Simone because if you did, you wouldn't do things like this."

"But, Tony—"

Her husband held up his hand to stop her. "You could have told me long before, Sim, you know you could have. I don't understand why you are so reluctant, so resistant to the idea of sharing more of yourself, your work, your life with me. I'm your husband—doesn't that mean anything?"

Simone nodded mutely, now aware of the deep pain in her husband's voice. She tried to speak, but the words wouldn't come. Her tongue stuck to the roof of her mouth. Why was he so bent out of shape? She'd taken speaking trips before...why was he so upset now? Deep down she could sense his disappointment in her, and it hurt.

"It seems to me," Tony went on, "that you take some kind of pleasure in hurting me with these unexpected bombs you drop. Simone," he pleaded, "don't destroy what we have. You are so smart, so clever in some ways and, I don't know, so stupid in other ways." He sighed and leaned back in his chair, as if to increase the distance between them.

"Tony, I meant to tell you before, way back, but so many things...we got caught up in—"

"Yeah, I know. But you have to be honest, Sim, most of these things you started."

"I'll take the blame for most of it, Tony. Guess I've been partly to fault, but not all, I won't say it's all my fault."

"How long will you be in California, anyway?"

"Only four days."

In a matter-of-fact voice, Tony continued, "Call me when you get there, and I will pick you up at Logan Airport when you get back to Boston."

Tony resumed taking a sip of his brandy, and Simone's mind went back to something her mother had said about the role of a woman in her man's life.

As Simone remembered it, the conversation took place the eve of her wedding. Her mother had remarked on how wonderful she thought Tony was.

going to be a wonderful husband, I just know it, He's so warm, gracious, and thoughtful, and a doctor. I'm sure his patients just love him. And the best part, he adores you. How did you happen to find such a treasure?"

"Well, you know, Mom," Simone answered with a wide grin, "you didn't raise no fools, and when I met Tony I knew he was the one. You said 'get the best,' and that's what I did. Isn't he perfect?"

Simone remembered how she had hugged herself and danced around the room with glee. Then she had stopped in front of her mother's chair and dropped to her knees.

"I'm so glad that you and Dad like him. I aim to have a perfect marriage, just like you two."

"Well, now, that will take work, honey. But I know you're not afraid of hard work. It takes a good woman to make a good marriage. Oh, sure, a woman should be independent, aware of herself, have strong self-value—but then, when these things are reflected in her husband's perception of her, he becomes stronger, more certain of his own worth because of what she brings into the marriage."

"What do you mean, really, Mom?"

"I mean it's the balance of the two personalities that makes a marriage unshakable. Neither of you is more important than the other—each is an independent entity, but it's the union, the oneness of the two that counts. And that, my dear child, can be hard work."

"I can do it," Simone said quickly as she stood and dropped a light kiss on her mother's head.

"I hope so," her mother answered.

CHAPTER IX

"Yes, Mrs. Housner, we have a reservation for you."

The registrar accepted her identification and continued in a mellifluous, artificial voice. "Your reservation was made by the Evans, Engret, and Rogers Company. I hope everything will be satisfactory."

"I'm certain it will be," Simone told him. "That's the company I'm making a presentation for tomorrow. I believe it's to be a dinner meeting here in this hotel."

"That's correct, ma'am. It's listed on our functions calendar. Someone will be here presently to take your bags. Enjoy your stay, and again, welcome to San Francisco." He smiled pleasantly.

She had received a warm welcome earlier at the airport. When she went to the baggage claim to get her luggage, a uniformed young black man waited with a sign that read, *EE&R Company Welcomes Mrs. Simone Harper-Housner.* Simone asked him the name of the company president, and when he said, "Mr. Benjamin Wales, ma'am," she allowed him to take her bag. He led her to a limousine and opened the door. Such luxury! The upholstery was plush grey velvet. Complete with a wet bar, ice, soft drinks, a small TM a pull-out desk, and a cellular phone, the limo defined efficient elegance. Simone stretched her legs in relaxed comfort as the driver closed the door.

"This is Mr. Wales' private car, ma'am," he said. "I'll take you right to the hotel."

Simone smiled to herself. When she had negotiated the contract for the seminar some months ago, she had wondered whether $2,500 plus her air fare was too much to ask for—but now she was happy that she had researched EE&R. It had turned out to be one of the country's top 100 successful black computer companies.

Her hotel accommodations were included in her expense account, and she was not disappointed when the limo pulled up in front of the beautiful, Spanish-type building and made a smooth stop at the canopied entrance. A uniformed doorman opened the limousine door and welcomed her.

The lobby was decorated in marble, lots of brass, and soft rugs, with a sparkling indoor water fountain in the center of the room. Low, comfortable chairs were placed in intimate groupings around the fountain. A glittering, shimmering chandelier was reflected in the water, and the soft tapestries on the walls muted the noise of the lobby activity.

On the desk of glossy wood and brass stood a magnificent arrangement of birds of paradise, orchids trailing over wood, and eucalyptus branches. There were pots of flowers and small decorative trees everywhere. It was a cool and welcoming room for the weary traveler.

Simone was stunned when she saw her accommodations—a suite of rooms. For two nights? She saw a huge bedroom with a king-size bed, a lovely sitting room that looked out toward a marina with white sailboats bobbing in the water, a balcony with comfortable rattan furniture, and a tiny glass table.

Besides the living room and bedroom, each with its own TV she noticed a small kitchen. In addition to the usual appliances, a fully stocked bar was revealed under the counter. Creamy beige marble walls with a Jacuzzi whirlpool bath defined the opulent bathroom, with thick beige and green towels draped over a heated bar. Large mirrors seemed to be everywhere, and rows of soaps, lotions, and colognes lined the marble sink top.

"There must be a mistake," Simone told the bellhop.

"No, ma'am. This is the right room."

Well, Simone thought, *EE&R must really have it to throw out the red carpet like this. But then, I try to do a professional job, so I guess I'm worth it.*

When she went downstairs to dinner that evening, she spied a poster on an easel outside one of the function rooms.

"I'll be blessed!" she spoke aloud. "It's me!"

One of her publicity pictures was on a cardboard display, framed by a gold and black border.

The Juliana Room
Simone Harper-Housner
Consultant from
Harper-Housner Financial Consultants, Inc.
Will Speak on
"How You Can Have a Safe and Sound Financial
Future Despite Troubled Waters"
Presented by
Evans, Engret, and Rogers Computers
Benjamin Wales, President and CEO
Cocktails: 5:30-6:30 p.m. Dinner: 7 p.m.
Speaker: 9 p.m.

As she read the poster, Simone hoped that she'd be over her jet lag by tomorrow. She'd better get to bed early tonight.

Later that night as she stretched out in the king-size bed with the sheets cool and relaxing against her skin, she thought of Tony.

She had called him before she went to bed, but true to his medical lifestyle, he was neither at home nor in his office. At some patient's bedside, she guessed. She left a message.

She snuggled deep under the covers in the large bed, mindful of its size and how lonely she felt. Her last thought before she fell asleep was, *We'll have to come to some decision soon about our marriage.* The uncertainty of their relationship caused only confusion and unhappiness for each of them.

For her dinner speech the following evening, Simone wore her electric-blue suede suit. Desiring a sleek corporate look, she wore grey suede pumps, and for her jewelry, pearl and gold earrings, her wedding gift from Tony. A blue-green silk scarf fastened with a gold brooch completed her outfit.

Her hair was smooth and shiny, and she had pulled it to the top of her head with a clip to give her more height. Her makeup had been artfully applied, a soft blush with a rose-hued tint on her cheeks and lips. She had outlined her eyes with black mascara. They seemed huge and innocent. She checked herself out in the mirror. *Okay, kid, go and get 'em!*

She was pleased with herself and very anxious to do a super job. Would Tony be proud of her tonight?

CHAPTER X

The Juliana Room was located on the hotel's second floor. As Simone rode up the escalator, she was impressed by the number of well-groomed African-Americans she saw. Their muted conversation indicated enthusiasm and eager interest as they made their way to the room.

Simone felt justified in the considerable sum she would be receiving for this trip. This was, after all, one of the country's most successful black companies. *Well,* she thought, *maybe I do deserve that fancy suite. But I really wish Tony were here to share it with me.*

She noted a tall man, about forty, walking toward her as she stepped into the Juliana Room.

Hands outstretched, he asked, "Mrs. Harper-Houser? I'm Marcus Baines, vice president in personnel. How are you?" Simone looked into a pair of friendly, dark brown eyes, grasped the extended hand, and shook it firmly.

"Are you comfortable here in the hotel?" he asked.

"Mr. Baines, everything has been just great. I hope I can give your company what you want. And, Mr. Baines, in my professional life, I'm known as Ms. Simone Harper." She smiled at him, "Makes it easier."

"Very well, Ms. Harper. We're looking forward to your talk, and we hope we'll have some time for Q&A."

"Mr. Baines, I always find the question-and-answer period of any meeting invaluable. Then I can evaluate my audience's reaction."

"I agree," he said as he walked her to the head table. "You'll be seated next to me, and I'll make your introduction. Do you need to check the mike?"

"Don't think so. My voice usually carries well, and this room..." she glanced around.

"We've used this room before. The acoustics are good, and there's usually a sound engineer available."

As Simone took her seat, she heard soft music in the background. Over to her left was a small dais. She noticed a set of drums, a piano, and a saxophone, each played by a woman of color. Good for EE&R—a company that believes in equal opportunity for the sexes, she thought. She recognized one of the Beatles' toe-tapping melodies.

She could see that the room was elegant, without being too cool or formal. The walls were covered with a sea-water green, damask-like material. The light came from well-placed, moderately sized chandeliers, dimmed at the moment. About twenty tables with seats for ten persons each were set with deeper green linen tablecloths. Place settings of mauve napkins, tasteful silverware, and delicate glassware added to the serene good taste of the room. A colorful bouquet of pink roses, anemones, and white carnations was arranged in a glass bowl on each table. The head table where Simone sat had settings for eight people. Company officials, she guessed.

The room filled rapidly. Simone took a moment to assemble her reminder cards. She had written down words, phrases, and important points she wanted to remember. She rarely wrote her speeches; she felt more relaxed, almost as if in conversation with the audience, without reading the speech.

"I don't know how you do it," Tony told her once after he heard her speak before a group of businesswomen. "If I were giving a talk like that, I'd have to have every word written down so I could read it. You're really smart—you know that, don't you, Sim?" He smiled at her. She saw his love for her in his eyes. As she looked over her cards, she felt warm and cared for as she recalled the moment.

She sensed Mr. Baines at her side.

"We are going to get started soon, Ms. Harper, but first I want to introduce you to the other head table guests. Oh," he indicated a bulky, middle-aged man of dark coloring, "Mr. Wales, our president."

Simone expected the man's voice to be a deep baritone-bass timbre, and it was.

"Good evening, Ms. Harper." His voice washed over her, almost enveloping her, it seemed. But the hand he offered was distastefully soft and fleshy.

Simone withdrew her hand quickly as she turned to speak to the man's wife.

"May I present my wife, Mrs. Wales, Ms. Harper."

Simone smiled at the small woman, a pale, plain-looking person who gave Simone a tentative smile and nodded. The other head table guests included, besides Mr. Baines' secretary, the company treasurer and the vice president in charge of research and development. There was another man at the table who was mentioned as being in charge of personnel, but he did not approach her. Simone didn't really get his name, but for some reason he seemed familiar to her.

The meal was exceptional and served in a quiet, restrained manner. Simone had expected no less than the best, and she was pleased with everything. She realized that she hadn't had a good meal in some time, not since the past weekend meal on the road to Vermont.

Smoked salmon on toast points was served with champagne. The main course of roast beef, thinly sliced, was offered with tiny boiled new russet potatoes. Garlic breaded, stuffed mushroom caps accompanied the entree. Simone relished the watercress and hearts of palm salad. The dressing of light oil and vinegar with a delicate hint of lime and tarragon delighted her. Her sense of well-being and comfort continued. Dessert was Bartlett pears that had been poached in Burgundy wine. A rich demitasse and red wine ended the meal. Simone sipped only the coffee. Soon it would be her turn to speak. As she waited, she made agreeable small talk with her dinner partners: Mr. Baines, who was really very nice, she thought, and Mr. Wales on her other side, who appeared pretentious and flamboyant. How had a person with that type of ego succeeded in the business world? Simone wondered what was truly behind this overbearing man.

Her talk went well. She spoke for about twenty minutes. The audience seemed receptive. After the applause, she began to field the questions from the group.

One young man asked for tips on reducing his tax liability. Simone laughingly told him that he had asked the most frequently asked question when people talked to a financial planner. "However," she said, "I would have to meet with you to determine your actual financial picture. But any library should have general information on tax strategies that can be adapted to your particular situation. And," she added, "the IRS does put out guidelines for each tax year, and these are available to the public."

"Next question?" She saw in the far reaches of the room a young man approach the mike that had been set up to accommodate those in the back of the room.

As the man started to speak, Simone felt her heart jolt. He looked like Tony! For a fleeting moment, she thought Tony had somehow followed her to California! Of course it was not her husband. But the same coconut-brown skin, the same wide shoulders, the same aggressive positive stance when he stood at the mike reminded her of her husband. She heard the young man speaking, but she couldn't understand him. She could scarcely believe that just the unexpected sight of someone who resembled her husband could create such panic in her. She raised her hand to stop his question.

"Sir, I'm sorry. Would you mind…starting again? Repeat your question, please?"

She needed the extra moment to compose herself. She desperately hoped that no one had noticed her momentary lapse in concentration.

"My question, Ms. Harper, concerns the future. Do you think the new European common market is going to help or hurt the economic picture in this country? What are you advising your own clients?"

God, he even sounded like Tony. Simone grasped the lectern with both hands, took a deep breath, and swallowed before she responded.

"Your question is a good one. I believe in preparing for the future as much as is humanly possible. Because the European borders are opening, trade barriers are disappearing and a new economy is being born in Eastern Europe. The former Communist Bloc nations need goods and services. History is being made with unification, and many investment opportunities are being offered. As to my clients, I am suggesting that they look into the New Real German Fund. More than twelve million shares are being offered, and I tell them to consider German steel, ceramics, wines, and electronics, among other things."

Simone saw pencils busily taking notes at her last remarks. She was relieved when Mr. Baines interrupted her. Her legs were weak with the tension she hadn't realized she felt.

"Ladies and gentlemen, we have time for one more question, then we'll have to adjourn."

He pointed to a young woman who caused a slight titter with her question.

"How can I save money—build up my assets—when I have bills to pay, like my college tuition?"

Simone nodded her head.

"You are not alone. To begin with—and that's the key, *begin with*—start a savings account. It need not be much, but put something aside each pay period. Be consistent. Don't touch your savings. Pay at least a little something on each of your bills. Again, it's being regular that counts.

Some consultants advocate consolidating your bills—taking out a loan to pay them off, and thus having only one monthly bill to pay. I don't advise that. Seems to me you are letting the control, the management of your affairs, fall into another person's hands. I'd personally feel better doing it myself, my way."

Then Mr. Baines closed down the questions and thanked Simone for a successful presentation. She felt intensely exhilarated by the crowd's applause.

She continued to accept congratulations as many people came forward to speak to her. She handed out business cards to those who requested them.

Suddenly she became aware of someone standing nearby, someone who seemed to move when she moved. She turned quickly when she felt a hand grasp her elbow.

"Simone, have time for an old friend?"

Recognition came slowly, then Simone gasped.

"Dayton Clark. What are you doing here?"

"I knew you didn't recognize me," the young man said as they shook hands.

CHAPTER XI

Despite Simone's original misgivings, they talked for some time. She glanced at her watch.

"Do you know it's almost eleven-thirty?"

He grinned at her. Simone remembered how, at one time, that mischievous grin had made her heart flip-flop. Dayton's olive-brown skin was still flawless in its texture. His close-cropped, dark brown hair outlined his perfectly shaped head.

No longer the skinny, awkward teenager she had seen ten years before, his well-sculpted muscles filled out his dark suit. Unspoken self-assurance enhanced his masculinity, and sparkling white teeth were revealed in his charming smile.

"Look, it's early, Simone. What say I come up to your room and we really get back to old times?" Dayton bounced his eyebrows up and down in an attempt at a lustful leer.

"Out of your mind, Day. I'm an old married woman now, you know." She laughed.

"Uh, well, I don't know about that." He took both her hands in his. She could sense a change in his mood. She shivered slightly.

"Hey, Simone...suppose we are still married..."

She pulled her hands from his grasp. "Man, what are you talkin' about? Still married?" Her eyebrows became twin question marks. "You know darn right well our folks had the thing annulled. I still have the paper."

"Yeah, I know," Dayton peered into her questioning face. "But suppose...just suppose...the judge wasn't a legal judge, hadn't been sworn in, lost his right to practice law, something like that."

"Dayton Clark, don't be silly, you are just grasping at straws. At any rate, it was a long time ago, and we were underage and, and..." She was getting angry. "Besides, we never slept together!"

"Something I've always regretted, my love, but it's not too late. Let me come up," he begged.

"Okay, Dayton, now let's be real. It was nice seeing you again." She pushed her half-finished glass of sherry away and began to gather her purse and the evening's program. She planned to show it to Tony when she returned home.

"Look, I'm glad we were able to spend this time together but, sweetie, as our former president said, 'Read my lips.' I'm going back to Boston in the morning. Back to my husband."

Up to that very moment, Simone was not sure that she would be returning to Tony. Now she had verbalized it. Had her subconscious mind made that decision?

She was unprepared for the alarm she felt when Dayton grabbed her hand as if to detain her. He held her left hand with both of his and began to twist her diamond ring and her wedding band around her finger.

"Just think, these could have been *my* rings you're wearing."

Now she was really exasperated. "Dayton, good night! Take care of yourself." She pulled her hand quickly from his grasp.

She did not look back, but left him standing at the table. She hurriedly made her way to the wall of elevators. This chance meeting was making her recall the whole regretful incident of her impulsive elopement with the man she'd just left.

She and Dayton were both eighteen years old that graduation night. At four in the morning, after the prom and after their hasty trip to the justice of the peace across the state line, they had returned to her home. Lights blazed from every room of her parents' house. She and Dayton walked to the front door, which opened before they got to the first steps.

Simone's father spoke in a low voice, obviously struggling to control his anger. He ignored his daughter and spoke directly to Dayton.

"Dayton, I've been on the phone with your folks. They'll be here in a few minutes. I suggest that you and..."

Simone saw her father briefly glance at her.

"I suggest that you and my daughter sit in the living room. We'll discuss nothing until your parents arrive."

Her father's calm, icy manner frightened Simone. Where was her mother? Her sister and brother? She knew everyone in the family was up, anxious to know what she had done. What seemed to her to have been an adventuresome lark two hours ago now seemed really stupid. How could she redeem herself, especially to her father?

Simone's relationship with her father had always been special to her. They had spent more time together and done more fun things together than her other siblings. She valued her father's opinion, and she loved him. She loved her mother, too, but she adored her father. The notion that perhaps now she had wounded him in his heart upset her. Would he ever forgive her for this foolish act that now, sitting here in the living room, seemed so stupid? In the truth of morning, Dayton looked so unglamorous, so thin, so young. Would things ever be right with Dad?

After the angry Clarks had come and gone and taken a penitent Dayton with them, Simone's mother came into the living room.

Mrs. Harper, a tall, large-boned woman, possessed an innate grace that made her very attractive. However, her eyes, hazel-green and set deep in her ivory cream-colored skin (bequeathed from a Caucasian ancestor) created her most striking feature: eyes that would take on a greenish-gold patina whenever she was emotional. Her reddish-brown hair, usually well-groomed, revealed in its wild disarray the depth of her concern for her daughter. Simone could read the signs. *You're in for it now,* she thought.

"This has been some night, Simone," her mother said. "It's not over yet."

Simone's knees shook, and her hands perspired as she clasped them together in her lap. She looked at her mother.

"Go take a shower and get into your night clothes. I'll be in to talk after you get into bed. I must..." Her voice quavered slightly, then picked up to a stronger pitch. "We, you and I, must talk tonight."

As she rode the elevator to her room, Simone's skin warmed and perspiration broke out on her upper lip as she recalled that "growing-up" incident, now seemingly ages ago.

Her mother had positioned herself at the foot of the bed and had leaned over to take Simone's trembling hands in hers.

Simone wished her mother would hurry and get this lecture over! Get this crazy night over. *We only got married; we didn't do anything else!*

Her mother spoke.

"Honey; I know, deep in my heart, that this getting married thing was your idea, wasn't it?"

Simone had nodded.

"That little ole' skinny Dayton Clark never did have much grit. He's so crazy 'bout you, he'd jump off the Brooklyn Bridge. Putty in your hands. Right?"

Simone kept nodding, speechless in the knowledge of her mother's wisdom.

"I know why you did it, too," her mother had continued. "Oh, I know I'm only a high school English teacher, but I'm your mother and I know my children. Especially you, my dear. You've always wanted to be first. Isn't that right?"

For the first time that night, tears had welled up in Simone's eyes.

Her mother went on, ignoring Simone's tears. "Your sister Cleo is a beautiful girl. You are, too. You are eighteen and she is twenty. I know...she has lots of lovely boyfriends. But, Simone, being jealous of your sister will not help you, ever, not at all."

How did her mother know of her envy for her beautiful older sister? she wondered.

Her mother had risen from the foot of the bed and pushed Simone toward the center of the bed. She climbed in beside her daughter and, when she had gathered the trembling girl in her arms, placed Simone's head on her chest.

Simone had not been held like that since as a child she'd had a strep throat.

"Look, my child, you've always been stubborn and willful. Your father and I never tried to take that from you, because a strong will and determination are good things—but someday that same stubbornness and hardheadedness can get you in trouble. They will also help you face many of life's battles. But you must also be flexible and wise. And," she spaced her next words carefully, "you...have...no...need to be jealous of your sister. You thought if you got married before she did, you'd be first. But, honey, no matter how hard you try to change things, you'll always be my second child. I don't love you less, Cleo less, or Dana less. My heart is big enough and has room enough for your Dad and each one of you kids."

Her mother chuckled and said, "If I should have three more of you kids—and that's not going to happen, believe me—I'd have room in my heart for them, too!"

Mrs. Harper had caressed her daughter's cheeks with her fingers and nuzzled the girl closer to her chest. This night, thinking about that night many years ago, Simone remembered how comforting her mother's touch had felt.

"Life," her mother had continued, "is meant to flow with expectations, goals, and triumphs. That gives a quality to one's life; that makes it unique and special. You don't have to knock it over the head and rush about trying to force things to happen—do you understand what I'm trying to say?"

Again, Simone nodded without speaking. Ashamed of her reckless action, she realized that her mother was right. Indeed, the idea to get married had been hers, so that she could be the first of the children to do one big thing. She liked Dayton, and he would do anything she asked.

"Your Dad," her mother continued, "has been on the phone all night. It's a good thing we have a friend who's a lawyer. He will take care of the necessary papers for the annulment. Dad says he can't talk to you tonight, but to tell you good night."

Simone had desperately wanted to see her father that night to let him know how sorry she was about the whole shameful incident. Her father never came. She had cried herself to sleep. Tonight's events brought everything back.

When she reached her room, she pulled her key out of her purse. Perhaps a soothing bath in the Jacuzzi was what she needed. Her nerves were taut, and she felt trembly inside. Giving the speech, answering the questions, the chance meeting with someone from the past, Dayton...and the memories of that teenage fiasco and her recent fight with Tony. No wonder she felt tense.

She had just unbuttoned her jacket to remove it when she heard a knock on the door. She rebuttoned it hurriedly before she spoke. That dumb Dayton! It was already midnight. She pulled the door open and said angrily, "Dayton, I said 'Good night'!" But when she opened the door, it was not Dayton—it was someone else.

"Mr. Wales!" she said. The man smiling at her from the doorway was Benjamin Wales, president and chief executive officer at Evans, Engret, and Rogers. Simone knew her surprise showed on her face.

"May I come in?" he asked pleasantly. "I wanted to thank you, personally, for the outstanding seminar you presented, but you left before I had an opportunity to do so. I know it's very late."

"Well, I..." Simone was angry with herself for her hesitancy. "Yes, thank you, come in." She stepped aside. She couldn't help but note the presumptive manner the man showed. Deep in her psyche, Simone felt a threat of a sexual entrapment.

She saw a middle-aged man, probably fifty or fifty-two years old, who had evidently become accustomed to having what he wanted.

A large, dark-complexioned man, he wore an expansive bristle-like mustache, apparently to compensate for the thinning hair on top of his head that he combed to put a few strands over his bald spot. His navy-blue suit of fine Italian wool was impeccably tailored. He wore black leather slip-on loafers with a fringed tassel on the toes. The musky scent of male cologne was overpowering and somewhat distasteful to Simone.

Mr. Wales walked into the room and turned to Simone, who stood with her hand on the doorknob. Her mind raced. *I know what he's looking for. So that's why I have a suite of rooms. Simone, you dummy!*

"Mrs. Housner, is your suite all right?" He waved his arms about. "Have everything you need? Anything we can do to make you more comfortable?" He smiled pleasantly. He closed the door and walked toward the bar.

"Everything has been fine, Mr. Wales. I'm leaving in the morning, but I'm pleased with the way things went. I thought the group was most receptive." She wanted to maintain a businesslike attitude.

"Indeed, indeed, my dear." He turned a benign face toward her. "You gave them exactly what the company wanted. Our employees are apt to be upwardly mobile, young black people, and the company wants them to be able to manage their fiscal resources—to get into the mainstream of life in America. Take advantage of all opportunities. Don't you agree? When I saw you on TV on *Wall Street Week*, I knew you could reach our audience."

"Thank you, Mr. Wales," Simone said, her mind racing to forestall the man's obvious intentions.

"We try to be innovative. Well, since you don't need anything, seem comfortable, why don't we have a nightcap?"

The man actually rubbed his hands together and looked at Simone, his eyebrows raised.

"Oh, not for me, thanks, but help yourself." Simone waved her hand toward the bar. *After all,* Simone thought, *it's your bar, your suite of rooms.*

Simone watched in amazement as he helped himself at the bar.

"Sure you won't join me? A little cognac would help relax you, and you'd sleep like a baby." His round face turned a well-intentioned smile toward Simone.

He busied himself at his task, evidently secure in what he was doing.

"Oh, sit down, Mrs. Housner. Make yourself comfortable. This is your home away from home, you know." He moved away from the bar and took a chair opposite Simone's.

Astonished, Simone watched him actually kick off his shoes and lean back in the chair with a relaxed sigh.

"It's been a long day," he said.

The words and the implication of the situation provoked Simone into action.

She rose from her chair almost in one leap, strode to the door and opened it. "In that case, Mr. Wales, you'd better not plan on a long night!" Her voice was as firm as she could make it, because her insides were quivering with anger. "You'd better take your shoes and your drink with you."

"Are you sure?" He smiled benevolently.

Simone stood by the opened door. "As sure as I'm standing here with this door open, Mr. Wales." She tried to suppress her rage as she watched the man shrug his shoulders and slide his feet into his loafers.

"Could have been a lovely night, Mrs. Housner," he said in a sarcastic, jeering voice. "For both of us."

"Good night, Mr. Wales." Simone closed the door firmly and latched the bolt. She trembled with rage at herself for being so stupidly naive and gullible. What did she expect when she saw the suite of rooms? And she had prided herself on being able to judge people, especially men. After all, she worked in a predominately male field. She was angry at Mr. Wales, too. Why did he think she would welcome his advances?

She took off her shoe and threw it at the door.

What a night this had been! Was Tony right? How come lately she'd had these problems? What was she doing wrong? How come lately she hadn't been able to take care of herself? What had changed? Had marriage done this to her?

CHAPTER XII

Simone slept fitfully that night. She was incensed by the action of Benjamin Wales and his assumption that she would be a willing participant in his "little games." She could hardly wait for morning to arrive so that she could check out of her room, even though her flight back to Boston did not leave until around noon. The hotel had set aside a lounge for guests who wished to have a base from which to sightsee or to shop before going to the airport or the train station, so Simone checked her luggage with the desk clerk and proceeded out of the hotel.

On her arrival into the city, she had noticed several small boutiques near the hotel, and she decided to pick up a silk scarf for her friend Chris. She purchased a charming, hand-painted ceramic brooch that would be perfect for Mrs. Hazelitt. What about her husband? *Well,* she thought, *even though I'm upset with him, I can be generous enough for him to know that I do think of him. Perhaps I can find something in leather.*

When Simone boarded her flight to Boston, she observed that the plane was full, mostly business travelers. She settled into her seat with a book that she'd picked up at the airport newsstand. Perhaps she'd read, or perhaps she'd watch the in-flight movie. To her disappointment, the book turned out to be very boring, and the movie was one that she'd already seen. This was going to be a slow flight.

Just as well, she sighed, as she rested her head on the back of the seat and closed her eyes. She was anxious to get back home and to her much-needed confrontation with her husband. Now was a good time to think and to sort things out.

Her mind wandered back to a warm memory, the day that Tony had taken her to meet his mother. Mrs. Housner's house in New Jersey was located in a small college town. Tony said that sometimes his mother would provide temporary housing for students, particularly if they were from Africa. If support were needed, people always seemed to call on Tony's mother.

Simone smiled as she remembered the drive from Boston to New Jersey. Tony had told her about the time that he and his high school buddies knocked over the black lawn jockey statues in front of some well-to-do homes in town. His mother paid for his share of the damages after she had fussed with him for destroying other people's property.

"You have no right to disturb anything that doesn't belong to you!" He said she had angrily shaken her finger in his face. "What you and your friends did was low-down and shiftless, and you know I'm not raising my sons to be no-accounts!"

Tony told Simone that his mother kept up her harangue as she slammed pots and pans on the stove, angry with him for his behavior.

"Your dead father would turn over in his grave—he died wishin' an' hopin' that his boys would make it in this world. I've done all I know how to do, to see that you boys have what your father would have wanted for you! Working at that damn tailor shop isn't exactly child's play, you know. What's the matter with you, boy?"

Tony said he knew how mad his mother was but more than that, he told Simone, he heard disappointment and weariness in her voice. Tony told Simone that his tongue stuck to the roof of his mouth, in a combination of dismay and embarrassment.

"Ma," he said, his throat tight with emotion, "I didn't mean to do anything. It was just being with the guys, and..."

"Bein' with the guys, huh?" His mother broke in. "If I have to work at that damn hell-hole of a shop pressin' n' cleanin' clothes 'til I die you boys are goin' to 'mount to something!"

Then, Tony told Simone, his mother ordered him to bed and told him that she would have his punishment lined up for him in the morning.

Tony said that he gave a sigh of relief. He could take his punishment, if only his mother wouldn't do that praying thing.

"Praying thing? What was that?" Simone wanted to know.

Tony shook his head and chuckled.

"I've told you, my dad died suddenly, I think from pneumonia. I was about twelve, and my brother Bart was ten. I'm not smiling because Dad died—it was a terrible time for all of us—but I'm smiling at the cleverness my mother always used in the face of adversity?"

"What do you mean, Tony?"

"Well, since we didn't have a father, my mother took God as her partner, literally. She would have impromptu prayer sessions to tell God all about the problems she faced with her sons."

"Out loud?" Simone questioned.

"Out loud, my love. With a son on either side of her, on our knees, she would pray for guidance and support."

"That must have made you boys shake."

"Did more than that. It kept us on the straight path. I can hear her now: 'Heavenly Father, I know you have given me these two special children to raise, and you know, oh God, I'm doing my best, but it's so hard alone with no husband to help me. Lord, you know I need your help. Just a little more help. Please, Lord.' "

Then Tony added, "That's when Mother would talk about the bad thing we had done, and we'd start to squirm. She'd hold us tighter so we'd know she really loved us—our faces would get all hot and flushed."

"I don't think I could have taken that, Tony."

"Well, what else could you do? You couldn't argue with your mother with God on her side, could you?"

"I guess not. Did she pray over you when you knocked over the statues?"

"No," Tony smiled at the memory. "I guess she thought the punishment she set up for me was sufficient."

"How did she punish you?" Simone wanted to know.

"I had to wash the kitchen floor, on my hands and knees, every week for a month. You know, 'cleanliness is next to Godliness', and I had to read four of the Great Books and give my mother a written report on each one. Of course she hadn't read them herself, but no matter, education was important. And," he blew out his cheeks, "I could *not* go to the Saturday night movies—my one vice, and then, to top it off, I had to do my brother's job of keeping the oil tank filled for the kitchen stove. A whole month of punishment."

"Did you do it?"

"Are you kidding? Of course I did. But Simone, the funny thing was what my mother said later. 'Was it worth all that punishment, Anton? You should have knocked down all those jockey statues in town. Left none of 'em standing!' " Tony grinned at the memory.

Half-dozing on the plane, Simone relived the feeling of graciousness and sincerity she had experienced that day when she met the woman who became her mother-in-law.

The memory of the tall, grey-haired, dignified woman filled her mind. Mrs. Housner had warm brown skin, unlined and serene. Her manner was calm and purposeful as she welcomed Simone into her home. The comfort and ease Simone experienced that weekend returned to her as she remembered her unmitigated happiness. Would she ever have that happiness again? Did she want it badly enough to work to attain it? Even if it meant changing herself? She wondered. Was she able to change? Her father had once told her, "If you can't change, you can't grow. And when you stop changing, you're dead—and that's when they throw the dirt in your face!"

Simone had expected Tony to meet her at the airport; instead, Mrs. Hazelitt showed up.

"I'm sorry," she said as she gave Simone a warm hug. "One of Dr. Housner's implant patients went into labor—they may have to do a Caesarean section. He had to stay at the hospital, so I said I'd pick you up."

"It's good to see you, Mrs. Hazelitt," Simone said as she linked her arm in the other woman's. Mrs. Hazelitt was on the plump side, and her comforting bulk felt good to Simone. It made her feel somewhat redeemed after the distasteful confrontation with Benjamin Wales. With Mrs. Hazelitt she felt validated, a little.

"Dr. Housner told me to get you home, and he promises to try to be there as soon as possible. The traffic is better now. It's almost eight, and I know," Mrs. Hazelitt said as she walked Simone to the parking lot, "with the time change and all, it's been a long day for you."

When they settled in the car and started to exit the airport, Simone thought to herself, *Just like Tony—making decisions for me—didn't ask me if I wanted to go home, just told Mrs. H. to take me there. Well, I am tired...and perhaps it's the right time to iron out our problem.*

By the time Mrs. Hazelitt drove up to the brownstone, Simone had made a decision. It might be best to put the past behind them and start over. She would have to try, because she did love Tony.

She invited Mrs. Hazelitt in for a cup of tea.

"No, my dear, I've got to get home. It's a bit of a ride to the South Shore where I live. Another time, perhaps."

"You know you're welcome," Simone said warmly. "And I want to thank you for picking me up."

"Anytime...anything for Dr. Housner. And you, too," she added hastily.

Nothing had been said about the disastrous ski trip. True to her word, Mrs. Hazelitt was a wise woman and did not bring up the subject. Nor did Simone, although it was on her mind.

In a way, she was glad to be home.

CHAPTER XIII

Simone showered and wrapped herself in her wooliest robe. She went to the kitchen and smiled when she saw the row of shiny new chrome canisters that Tony had evidently purchased. Somehow she didn't feel angry anymore. She made herself a cup of tea.

She took it with her to the living room and lighted the well-placed logs in the fireplace. Tony always said, "What's the use of having a fireplace if you don't use it?" He'd be happy to see it in operation this chilly evening, Simone thought.

She sat in one of the wingback chairs that flanked the fireplace. She rolled her head wearily along the back of her shoulders to relieve some of the tension. What approach should she take when she and Tony talked? It was not in her nature to be submissive, but if she wanted to keep her husband—and deep down in her heart she knew that she did—it would not do to be irritating. What she really wanted was his understanding. He should realize that she needed to be a strong woman—and she needed a strong man. If he could be strong without being dictatorial, it would be perfect. Strength attracted strength.

Tonight she looked around the room that she had finally come to love. Its peace and comfort came from seeing her collection of books side by side with her husband's in the ceiling-to-floor bookcase. Even the colonial-type, blue woven tapestry on the wingback chairs added to her contentment. She had not realized that it had become home to her.

Her own things had made the place home. Next to her chair stood a small cherry table that she had brought with her from Richmond. A white-shaded crystal lamp reflected radiantly on its glowing surface and on a small ceramic angel by Lladro that she had placed there. A fragment of delayed annoyance frayed her peace of mind. What would she be thinking tomorrow night at this hour after she and Tony had their talk?

Simone had just put down the teacup when she heard the phone ring in the den.

"Simone, my love, you're back!" It was Tony.

"Yes, Tony, I'm here."

"Did your trip go well?"

"Very well, I'm happy to say."

"Can't wait to see you. But I'm afraid I'm going to be a bit longer. Mrs. Hazelitt told you?" he went on, eagerness evident in his voice. "I'm not doing the section, another doctor is handling that, but I do want to be here to see how things progress. It's one of *my* babies..."

"One of your 'in vitros,' Mrs. Hazelitt said."

"Yes, this couple has waited almost 15 years for this baby. She is 38, and he's almost 40. So they are very anxious. I've got to stand by."

"Of course, Tony."

"As soon as the baby makes a three-point landing, I'm on my way home. Simone?"

"Yes, Tony?"

"I love you, girl." She could hear the tenderness in his soft voice.

She replaced the telephone receiver and walked slowly back to the living room. From Tony's tone of voice, it was as if there had never been discord between them. Almost as if nothing had happened. How did he plan for them to go on if they did not deal with the situation that had disturbed their peace? she wondered.

The telephone rang again, just as she bent to place more wood on the fire. She hurriedly replaced the fire screen and ran to the den. It might be Tony again.

"Hello?"

She heard a woman's voice with a strange accent.

"Is this the residence of Dr. Anton Housner?"

It was a dipped, British-sounding accent.

"This is Dr. Housner's residence. This is Mrs. Housner."

Simone did not recognize the voice.

"Oh, my, yes! How happy I am to speak with you. My name is Dr Miriam Urabjame. I wanted to thank Dr. Housner for the lovely dinner that we had again last evening. Would you please convey that message to him for me?"

"I'd be happy to," Simone said, aware of the flat effect that she hoped she conveyed to the caller.

"Oh, I do thank you, and hope to see you both soon."

Simone replaced the phone, a puzzled frown on her face.

Taken to dinner *again*, the woman had said. She sounded young and, from the name she had given, must be African. The accent surely indicated that. The name was not familiar to Simone.

So Tony's been taking women out to dinner Why did I think that he was sitting here in this brownstone, eating crackers, and drinking tea and sherry? Well, now!

She sat with her feet pulled up beneath her in the chair and stared at the fire. The quivering feeling in her stomach almost made her nauseous. Never, in God's green earth, did she imagine her husband to be unfaithful. Not Tony.

The logs on the fire crackled, and bits of broken wood sparked, fluttered, and colored white-hot into glowing embers. Somewhere in the den she heard the Seth Thomas clock, a gift from Tony's brother, strike off the hours. Nine o'clock.

Suddenly she wanted to leave the house—not be home when Tony came—but on the other hand, she needed to know the truth. She chewed her lower lip and drummed her fingers on the arm of the chair. She thought, *Whether or not you're ready, it's decision time, girl.* She went back to the telephone. She had to talk to someone.

Her friend answered the phone on the first ring.

"Chris? It's Simone."

"Hi, Simone. Glad you're back. Have a good trip?"

"Yes, it was a good trip. Made a good piece of change, too, glad to say. It was worth going. Made some contacts, you know."

"You're at the brownstone, I take it," Chris said.

"Chris, I've got to tell you," the words sprang from Simone's mouth, "some woman just called here. Dr. Miriam something, sounded like an African. Can you believe that?"

"What did she say?"

"Wanted to thank Tony for taking her to dinner. Here I thought he was missing me, trying to deal with our problems. At least that's what he told me! I'm working my tail off, taking all kinds of guff and nonsense..." a picture of Benjamin. Wales soared into her mind, as well as the meeting with Dayton, and increased her anger, "and he's enjoying himself!"

"Well, Simone, how long have you been away from Tony?" Chris asked in a calm voice.

"Makes no difference how long," Simone blurted. "He says he loves me, and we have a problem between us to solve. He should be thinking about that. Not taking some bimbo to dinner."

"If I were you, Simone, and I'm not, but you called me, if I were you, I'd take stock of what I had. Only you can make the decisions that will change the rest of your life."

"I know what you're saying, Chris. I guess deep down it's a need I have to control..."

Her friend's laugh stopped Simone in mid-sentence.

"It's not funny, Simone, but did you hear what you just said? 'A need to control.' That's what you've complained about in Tony, his need to control you. I'm laughing, friend, because you two are more alike than you know. You two were made for each other." She laughed again.

In the face of her friend's analysis, Simone said, "Chris, do you really think so?"

"I do. I never knew a couple like you. Both strong-willed and determined." She went on, "You know, Simone, I've known you a long time. You're a good friend, and I want you to be happy. Think about how Tony makes you feel about yourself."

"What do you mean, Chris?"

"Love is reflected in how your partner makes you truly feel. Tony doesn't take from you, he adds to you. His love for you gives you honor and acclaim because he chose you. You feel that way, too. I can tell."

"How?"

"You're more sure of yourself. You walk taller, seem stronger, even more assertive, not because you're Mrs. Anton Housner, but because your husband sees those qualities in you. Simone, it's like two halves of a whole that come together to make a single perfect unit. You're a lucky girl, my friend."

"Well, I guess, but I'm upset."

"What you are, kid, is *jealous* and that, my dear, is a good sign. Means that you care don't want to give up what's yours. You've heard the phrase, 'jealously guarded'?"

"Yes, of course."

"That's what you're doing now. Jealously guarding what you feel is rightfully yours. Guess you didn't know how much you loved your husband."

CHAPTER XIV

Simone returned to the living room and picked up her teacup. The tea was now cold and flat, but she was too upset to notice or to care what she drank.

The doorbell rang. Simone glanced at her watch. Almost nine-thirty. Who could it be? Tony had his own key, and besides, he said it would be some time maybe midnight before he'd get home.

She pulled her robe tighter around her waist, secured the ties, and padded to the door As she switched on the hall overhead light, she peered through the peephole. *My God, it's Dayton Clark!* Surprised, she released the lock and pulled open the door.

"Dayton, I just left you in California! What in the world are you doing here in Boston?"

"I came to see you, my wife."

Stunned, Simone blurted out, "Your *wife?* Dayton, what are you talking about? Are you crazy?"

She closed the door and glared angrily at the young man she had not expected to see again.

"How did you get my address? How did you find me?" She stammered, angry with herself for being placed in such an untenable situation.

"No problem, Mone." She recoiled at his use of his pet name for her when they were in high school. "Told you I was in charge of personnel at EE&R. No trouble at all to get your address from the company files."

Though visibly upset by Dayton's presence, Simone realized that she would have to take quick charge of the situation.

"Look, Dayton," she said in a no-nonsense tone, "I don't know why you're here. I know I'm not your wife, but come in the living room. I'll have to get some clothes on..."

"Don't have to change for me," he interrupted. "You look just great."

"In here." She pointed him into the living room. "Be right back."

She ran down to the bedroom and slammed the door. What did that idiot mean by "came to see his wife"? He's crazy!

She kicked off her slippers. Quickly, she pulled on underwear, a pair of black slacks, and a black-and-white, heavy turtleneck sweater before pushing her bare feet into loafers.

She'd have to get to the bottom of this. Could she get him out of the house before Tony came home?

One thing was for sure: This put a different picture on her reunion with Tony. She'd have to...well, get this Dayton mess cleared up. She always believed in facing problems head-on, a directness people often said got her into trouble.

Dayton stood with his back to her, looking at the books in the bookcase. Simone noticed his broad shoulders, a great change from the almost fragile, thin look he'd had as a teen. She plunged into the matter.

"Dayton, you're making a great mistake. I am certain we are not married. I don't know why you have the mistaken notion that we are."

He started to interrupt, but Simone stopped him with her hand upraised and spoke quickly, anxious to have her say.

"Where are you staying here in Boston?"

"I'm at the Ritz Carlton."

"Good, not far from my office. I can meet you…let's see," she tried to visualize her appointment calendar, "I can meet you at one-thirty tomorrow in the lobby. We can find a place to talk."

She propelled him to the front door and opened it.

"Can't say I'm pleased about this, Dayton. But we'll dear it up."

"Look, Mone," he insisted, "I'm not trying to cause trouble, but really we are still married. I know it."

"Tomorrow, Dayton, half past one in the lobby of the Ritz Carlton."

She pushed him out the door and flung herself back on the closed door. She shook her head as if to dear her mind.

Her homecoming with Tony was in jeopardy now. What to do? How could they come together with this new problem between them?

She picked up the phone in the bedroom and called Chris for the second time that night.

As she heard the phone ring, she glanced at her watch. Ten-thirty. She hoped Chris was up—she usually went to bed after the eleven o'clock news.

"Yes?"

"Oh, Chris. I'm glad you're still up. It's me again, Simone. I'll be over to your place in the next fifteen minutes. Can I stay for a few days?"

"Stay? What do you mean? You just got home. Isn't Tony there?"

"I'm expecting him later. Please, Chris, I'll explain everything...I'm in a big hurry."

"Well, okay, Simone. I hope you know what you're doing."

A half-hour later, Simone labored to explain her situation to her best friend.

"I left Tony a note telling him that I wanted a few more days to think out our problem. Told him I'm with you."

"Did you tell him about this nut, Dayton?"

"No, I didn't. Tony would only want to confront him, and I don't think that would work. Dayton is not the same quiet, unassuming boy I knew. There's something different about him. I told him I'd see him tomorrow. He's staying at the Ritz Carlton."

"You think that's wise?" Chris wanted to know.

"I'm going to call Connie, my secretary, first thing in the morning and check my calendar. I think I left it open, knowing I'd be just returning from the coast. I've got to straighten this thing out, Chris."

"Well, I guess so," her friend said. "Do you have copies of your annulment papers?"

"I know I do. I put them in our safety deposit box after Tony and I got married."

"My suggestion would be that you get them out and get over to your lawyer's office before you see the nut."

"Don't call him that, Chris. He was always a good kid."

"Ain't no good kid, now, honey, coming in and messin' up your life especially now," Chris stated firmly.

The phone rang, and both girls jumped, startled.

"Probably Tony," Chris said as she picked up the receiver.

"Yes, Tony," she raised her eyebrows and nodded to her bedroom where Simone could use the extension.

"Yes, she's here, one moment." She waited until she heard Simone pick up the receiver in the bedroom and as she hung up could hear Tony's voice booming.

"Simone, what in hell is going on? I thought…"

Chris hung up the phone and shook her head. Simone is going at this all wrong, she thought.

CHAPTER XV

"Tony's so angry with me. I think I've pushed his last button," Simone reported wearily to her friend when she returned to the living room.

"Do you blame him? What'd he say?" Chris asked.

Before she answered, Simone sat down on the couch and placed her head between her hands. Chris saw sadness in Simone's face when she raised her head to look at her friend.

"He says he doesn't understand me, and if I don't come home very soon, he's ready to call it quits—that he can't stand my changing my mind all the time."

"What did you tell him?"

"What could I say? Chris, I know I want to be with Tony. This past weekend has made me see that. But I must dear up this Dayton thing. I asked Tony to give me a few days, that's all. I didn't mention Dayton."

"Simone, haven't you forgotten something?" Chris had a serious frown on her face. "Didn't you go into your marriage ready to become *one?* Girl, you have a brilliant husband—a good and decent man. Don't deny him the right to help you. You should be a team. Why do you think you have to go it alone?"

Chris threw up her hands in mock disgust and continued.

"Simone, you're my friend and I hate to say this, but with all the education and degrees you have, you don't have what the old folks called 'mother-wit.' You know what I mean, good common sense!"

"Maybe you're right, Chris."

"I know I am! There's nothing more satisfying than to be a part of a team working together to solve a problem. Let Tony help! You owe it to him, after all you've put him through!"

Chris' voice softened. "Don't mean to be hard on you, kid, but..."

"I know, I know," Simone interrupted, picked up her overnight bag, and headed down the apartment hall to the guest bedroom.

She turned halfway down the corridor and went back to the living room.

"Chris, did I remember to say thanks?"

"Pshaw, don't worry, kid. Just try to get some rest. You must be worn out." She turned to Simone. "Want anything from the kitchen?"

"No thanks, Chris, the kitchen's not my favorite part of the house," Simone said as she closed the bedroom door behind her.

Sleep was a long time coming for Simone—and when it did, it was a fitful sleep, full of weird dreams and nightmares. She dreamt that she and Tony were on a Caribbean island, walking hand in hand, barefoot on the white sand. Occasionally the waves would reach up and overtake their feet, and they would jump, childlike, out of the cold water. The sun was warm and gentle on their skin, and Simone felt so loved and cared for that she could barely tolerate the joy she experienced. Suddenly in her dream, as she and Tony progressed down the beach, a group of young natives came toward them. They seemed to be heading to the breakwater just behind the couple. They carried picnic baskets, jugs, umbrellas, and cartons of beer. "Going to have a good old 'jump-up,' " Simone told Tony. As soon as the group came abreast of Simone and Tony, they turned. The picnic baskets became machine guns, the umbrellas fierce-looking military weapons—Ak-47s—and the men demanded of Tony, "Give us your woman, man, or we take her!"

As she and Tony started to run, she tripped and fell face down on the hot sand. She screamed, "Tony, Tony, help me!"

She sat bolt upright in bed. Where was she? It seemed an eternity before she realized that she was not in San Francisco, not at the brownstone, but in her friend Chris' guest room.

Still shaken from the nightmare, she got up, put on her bathrobe, and went to the kitchen. Quietly, so as not to wake Chris—after all, she had to get to work in the morning—she poured herself a glass of milk and scouted for cookies.

When she found some crackers, she put a few on a plate, picked up the glass of milk, and returned to her room.

The dream still seemed real. *Maybe Chris is right. Perhaps I do need Tony to help me this time. I surely was calling him in my dream wonder if my subconscious is trying to tell me something. What was it Momma used to say, "Don't be hardheaded all your life!" and Daddy would say, "Know when you can go it alone, but also know when to ask for help."*

And now, because of her pigheadedness, she was in this trouble.

As she sat in the dark room, she munched the crackers—tasteless and dry—and took a few sips of the cold milk. She hoped she could get back to sleep. She looked out the window and watched the cars move up and down the street. The headlights flickered, grew brighter as they approached the apartment building, then faded as their red taillights winked out of sight. She noticed that one of the trees across the street seemed unusually bumpy along one side. Simone stared at the dark trunk and thought she saw a slight movement. She got up and peered closer, thankful that the room was dark. Just then a car neared the building, and she could see more clearly.

She could see that it was a person in dark clothing. It was man, looking directly at Chris' apartment. Who was watching her?

CHAPTER XVI

Amanda Clark had worried constantly about Dayton. Preston, her husband, repeatedly warned her about her overindulgence of their son.

"Give him room," he'd bark at her in his no-nonsense, gruff voice. "Leave him be! He's got to make his own mistakes. Stop tryin' to make the world perfect for him."

His words went unheeded, and Dayton could scarcely recall a day while he was growing up that his parents weren't discussing him. It made him feel suffocated, as if he couldn't breathe in that atmosphere.

Amanda Clark adored her only child. Never during her spinster years had she ever dreamed she would have such a treasure…a beautiful child to love. She loved everything about him, especially the clean, sweet smell of the child's body. To bathe him, smooth his strong, sturdy brown arms and legs with baby lotion, was almost too pleasurable to bear.

When the doctor had placed her newborn infant in her eager, unbelieving arms, Amanda was 38 years old and had been married for ten months to Preston Clark, a plain-faced, robust, dark-skinned man. They had noticed each other every day on the bus ride to the city. The forty-minute ride gave each of them time to size up the other.

One day, Preston got bold enough to actually take the empty seat next to Amanda. She looked up from her book to acknowledge his presence with a brief nod, but quickly returned to her reading. It took another week of respectful silence before Preston spoke. She had finally closed the book.

"My momma allus said, 'A woman with clean, shiny hair is a real true woman,' 'n you got the cleanes', shinies' hair I ever seen."

A preacher friend of Amanda's widowed mother married the couple in the front room of her mother's small apartment. Amanda had packed her few belongings and moved into Preston's apartment over the gym.

She hated the place. She could never get rid of the masculine smells of the gym. Odors like sweat, liniment, and other noxious smells permeated the walls of the small rooms that she and her husband shared. She washed constantly.

"Stop washing so much, woman," Preston would complain. "Walls be down to bare wood, you done scrubbed off so much paint. Little dirt never hurt nobody."

But it was as if Amanda could not be clean enough. "Cleanliness nex' to Godliness," she would say and tighten her lips into a prim line.

"I know wha' the Good Book says," he would retort, "but too much of anything ain't good. Shouldn't be washin' so much all the time. Takes all the oils out the skin, so much washin' all the time. Ain't never been nothin' wrong wi' the good smell o' hones' sweat. Means a man done hard, hones' work."

But he knew he'd better wash and change his clothes before he sat down to the dinner meal.

The whole thing got worse as the child grew. "Stop tryin' to dress the boy like a sissy," he'd bark at her. "Fa God's sake, let him get dirty!"

Amanda would quietly gather the small child protectively in her arms and ignore her husband. He knew she never heard him. He felt he'd have to wait until the boy was older before he could have some say in the matter. "Goin' ruin him, jes' ruin him." He would leave, frustrated, and seek solace in his all-masculine world downstairs in the gym.

Dayton found his freedom and relief outdoors, on the track field at the high school, where he and Simone got to know each other. Each wanted to succeed for different reasons.

Dayton worshipped Simone from the start. Because her father was the high school principal and a person involved in community activities, and because his father ran a small gym in the seedy part of the city, a social gap existed between the pair. To Dayton, Simone Harper seemed unattainable, out of his reach until that fateful prom night.

He could hardly believe it when she had actually suggested they run off and get married. He'd been excited just to hold her in his arms as they danced and to be able to breathe the heady intoxication of her perfume.

Dayton recalled the rage and humiliation his father showed, banging his hands on the steering wheel as they drove home from the Harper house.

"Boy," he asked between terse lips, "what in hell got into you? Those Harper people just know they're better 'n us, with all their educatin' 'n smarts."

His son could smell the sweet, onion-like odor coming from his father's sweaty, damp undershirt. His father never dressed in a coat and tie, except for a wedding or funeral. Dayton was embarrassed by his mother's sobbing and whimpering as if the end of the world were at hand.

His father continued talking as they sped through the early dawn to their home on the other side of the city. "You'd better believe they don't want you in their family. 'Now, Mr. Clark,' his father had mimicked Simone's father, 'I have spoken to my lawyer. Of course, annulment proceedings will be started in the morning.' Can't wait to drop you, boy."

Dayton understood his father's feelings, and within himself he vowed that someday, somehow, he'd be a success so he could claim Simone as his.

Track scholarships were not as plentiful or as glamorous as football and basketball scholarships, but Dayton did his best. He tried out for the U.S. Olympic track team and won a spot for the high hurdles. Although he took no individual medals, he acquitted himself well enough to be noticed by the media as a potential future star. Finally he was recruited by the track coach at the University of Southern California. He got his bachelor's degree and finished his education with a master's in business administration from Stanford University. Armed with these credentials, he finally moved into his executive position at Evans, Engret, and Rogers Computer Company.

When at last he saw her that night in California, it was like an omen. Here she was, and she was supposed to belong to him. Why else would the gods have sent her all the way from Boston?

He arranged with his office for a two-week leave. Something about his parents needing him—an only child needing to settle some affairs for his aging folks.

"Sure, Dayton," his immediate supervisor, one of the company's vice presidents, had said. "You have never asked for much leave. If you can keep in touch with our office, take all the time you need. But you know we are up for a new contract. It will require rounding-up a cadre of skilled personnel, so we certainly would want you here for that piece of work. Sure, take the time."

"Thanks, Mr. Ormway. I will leave my schedule with my secretary, with phone numbers where I can be reached."

He had no intention of letting people know he was headed for Boston. He'd brief his mother. She'd know how to handle any calls. He could depend on her not to divulge his whereabouts, not even to his father, if Dayton asked her not to do so. His Mom had always been in his corner.

Tonight, in Simone's brownstone, he'd been pleased with the unbelieving look she showed when he told her he was staying at the Ritz Carlton. He'd had to control himself, bite his tongue, to keep from blurting out what he was thinking.

Yes, I can afford the Ritz!

Now it was close to midnight, and he lay on his bed in his hotel room to plan his next move. Wait until Simone met him the next day. She was in for a surprise, and so was that so-called big-time doctor husband of hers.

He got up suddenly from the bed, took off his robe, and went into the bathroom. After his shower, as he stood drying himself, he admired his muscular body. One thing about having a father in the gym business was the way a guy could keep his body in shape. His father had encouraged him, "Work at it, boy. Let those muscles develop. Pump up all you can! Never let a day go by 'thout you exercisin." His father was proud of his son's body. Dayton, too, realized that many women were attracted to him because of his impressive muscles. Southern California sunshine made him the envy of many pairs of eyes as he cruised the California beaches in his free time.

CHAPTER XVII

The welcome smell of freshly brewed coffee woke Simone. Chris set a steaming cup in front of her when Simone went to the table.

"I need this badly, Chris," Simone said as she sipped the hot liquid.

"I know. Had a bad night, did you?"

"Awful. Nightmares and...well..." Simone decided at the last moment not to mention the man she had seen last night. No need to upset Chris any more than she already had by barging into her life.

Chris spoke up.

"You know, Simone, I'm not sure it's a good idea for you to meet this Dayton character alone. It seems like a red flag to me that an old boyfriend would follow you, seek you out, you know, travel three thousand miles...I'm worried about your safety."

"Chris, I hear what you're saying, but I believe I can handle this situation. You know, I'm not the compulsive, headstrong girl I once was. Learning my business, dealing with other people's finances, has taught me to look carefully and closely at every side of an issue."

"Well," Chris wondered aloud, "what are you going to do?"

Simone sighed and leaned back in her chair. She saw the anxiety on her friend's face.

"First, as soon as I'm showered and dressed, I'm going to call Connie and tell her to cancel any appointments. As I said, I don't believe there are many because I knew I'd be tired from the California trip. Then I'm heading straight down to the bank to the safety deposit box. I'm going to make a photocopy of that blasted annulment, and then I'm calling Alex McRichards, our attorney. I hope he'll be available and not in some court session. I won't see Dayton at the Ritz until later, about one-thirty."

"What about Tony? Are you going to get in touch with him tell and him anything about this mess?" Chris' concern showed as she stood by the sink rubbing a dishcloth absentmindedly over the kitchen counter.

"Chris," Simone's voice was shaky, "I know deep in my heart that Tony is in my life to stay. I have been selfish, stubborn, and unable, in my stupidity, to realize how much he loves me. Not many men would have put up with my antics this long." She went to the sink to rinse out her coffee cup and turned to face Chris, tension visible in her face. "I made the mistake of eloping with Dayton, and if Dayton is confused about that, it's up to me to straighten things out with him. Tony has a lot on his mind right now. He's finally been invited to Paris to present a paper. He'll be leaving soon, and I can't saddle him with this mess now."

"Simone, you're only making the whole thing worse, believe me, by not sharing it with your husband. It would be a lot easier for you both if you did. And that, my dear, good child, is my last word on your problem. but promise me..."

"Promise you what?"

"Promise me that you will think about what I've said. Don't just blow it out of your mind."

"I promise, Chris. I really appreciate all that you've done for me."

"I only want you and Tony to be happy."

Tony! Simone's heart dropped as she thought of her husband. How long could she expect him to put up with her frenetic, crazy antics? Did he love her enough to patiently continue to suffer more setbacks and trials in their relationship? Damn that Dayton, she thought. Immediately an inner voice spoke. *Dayton didn't do it by himself, you know, stupid.*

Once during a high school track meet, Simone tripped over the last high hurdle and fell on the gravel path. Her face was badly bruised and lacerated by the bits of stone and dirt. The cornea of her left eye had bits of debris embedded in it. Treatment was successful, and no permanent scars remained. However, when tired or emotionally fatigued, Simone wore glasses. Not only did they help her vision, but they also made her seem a more responsible person, she sometimes thought.

She decided she needed the look to face Dayton. She had worn her russet challis skirt with a black wool blazer. Her gold silk blouse was complemented by a gold pin on the lapel of the jacket. Mr. McRichards' office was a comfortable, quiet room in one of Boston's leading bank buildings. The lawyer had welcomed her, offered coffee that she refused, and then asked, "How may I help you, Mrs. Housner?"

Simone explained her problem—somewhat embarrassed, but nevertheless eager to get the professional counsel she needed.

She watched the lawyer's face as he listened. His reddish-brown hair was carefully combed over a small balding area on the front of his head, and he nodded encouragingly as Simone told her story.

As he leaned forward to pick up a pen and draw a yellow legal pad forward, she noticed his well-groomed hands. His fingernails were squarish, with prominent white moons showing at the base of each. Tony often told Simone, "You can tell a great deal by looking at a man's hands. Well-kept and meticulously clean hands indicates a person who is careful, attentive, and conscientious. Most often you can trust such a person."

Simone felt the interest and care that she needed emanating from this man. She watched him review her documents.

He cleared his throat, dropped the pencil on the pad, and looked at Simone.

"Mrs. Housner, you need not worry. Your annulment is a valid one. A competent authority, the judge of the county seat, made the annulment legal. From what you have told me and what this copy indicates, the marriage had not been consummated."

Simone nodded.

"And," the lawyer continued, "the suit to annul the marriage was brought within a reasonable time, twenty-four hours, you say, so it would not be barred by laches."

"Laches?" Simone questioned.

"Laches. This is a term that means negligence in timely reporting of the complaint. It's a middle English term, *lachesse,* meaning a delay in establishing a right or a claim."

"Oh, no, there was no delay. My father's lawyer started proceedings the very next day."

"You say that this, uh, individual insists the annulment was not completed?"

"That's what he indicated to me."

"To you." Mr. McRichards raised his eyebrows as he waited for Simone's answer. "Your husband does not know?"

Simone took a deep breath before she responded.

"My husband knew about my annulment before we were married, Mr. McRichards. I have been out of town on a business engagement, San Francisco, to be exact, and that's where my...where Mr. Clark approached me. I really would like to get the matter resolved before I have to bother my husband with the question."

"I see."

"I feel that it was something that happened before we were married. It was my mistake—and I'd like to clear it up." Simone's palms were sweaty, and she could feel the perspiration moistening her armpits.

"Personal question, Mrs. Housner. You needn't answer if you don't wish to do so, but..."

Simone knew what the question would be, so she answered quickly.

"Mr. McRichards, yes, I do love my husband. Very much! Enough that I want only the best for him." Simone's eyes flamed with intensity as she spoke.

"I thought that would be your answer. But I must caution you, my dear, a good marriage is based on honesty—and I suggest you let your husband know about this dilemma. A united front is the best front. You say you have an appointment to see...Mr. Clark, is it..." he glanced at the notes on his yellow pad, "later today?"

"Yes, we are meeting at the Ritz Carlton at one-thirty."

"Tell you what. You go to the meeting. Try to find out from him what premise he's using to say you two are still married, what facts or information he has that makes him think that. Write it all down, document what he says, and get back to me. As I said at the outset, I don't believe he has anything. And, Mrs. Housner, be careful. He may be unbalanced. You are a very attractive woman, you know. So just be cautious."

The lawyer rose and extended his hand to Simone.

"My best to the doctor, and keep in touch."

Simone grasped the hand extended to her and shook it firmly.

"I'll do that, Mr. McRichards. Thank you."

As she left the lawyer's office she felt a little better, but not much. Everyone was urging her to tell Tony about Dayton. Maybe they were right. Perhaps this was one of the times her father said she would face. "Always know when to ask for help. Don't be proud and foolish."

CHAPTER XVIII

The lobby of the Ritz Carlton was bright and elegant. Quiet and serene, it spoke of years of influence and prestige as the grande dame of Boston's hotels. Simone noted the small glass showcases that exposed exquisite pieces of priceless jewelry and swatches of rare tapestries and silks. Each exhibit hinted at opulence of plenty and of wealth. Simone's heels clicked across the marble floor as she approached the registration desk. She was eager to get this meeting with Dayton behind her.

"Is there a message here for Mrs. Housner?" she asked the young blonde woman behind the desk.

"Right here, Simone." A man's voice came from the rear of the lobby.

Simone whirled around at the sound and saw Dayton coming through the lobby door.

A disarming smile was on his handsome brown face.

"Simone, you look great! Even with glasses."

Simone felt his eyes travel up and down her body approvingly as he took in her petite frame, her attractive haircut, and her enticing appearance. Simone almost wished she had worn less appealing clothes.

"Would you like to have lunch, Simone–or it's almost two p.m.... the tearoom is open. They serve tea from two to five o'clock here at the Ritz," Dayton told her.

He took her elbow and propelled her toward the staircase.

"I guess tea will be fine. I'm not too hungry." Simone's desire for food was tempered by her desire to get this confrontation over and done with as soon as she could manage it.

A formally dressed waiter showed them to a table, pulled out a chair for Simone, and, when she was seated, handed her a menu.

It took only a few minutes to order Earl Grey tea, cucumber sandwiches, and fresh scones with raspberry jam.

Simone went right to the subject on her mind. She looked directly at Dayton and asked him, "What makes you think we are still married? That the annulment is not legal? You've really upset me, you know."

She leaned back in her chair, expecting an explanation.

Dayton laughed, a cheerless, hollow sound that disturbed Simone.

"I don't have anything," he said quietly, watching her face for a reaction.

"Don't have *anything?* Well, what..." she sputtered, her anger and frustration almost rendering her speechless. She started to push back her chair to leave.

Dayton stayed her motion with his hand and tried to calm her down.

"Mone," he used his favorite name for her again, she noticed. She shook her head as if to shut out his voice.

"Mone, I'm sorry, but it was something I had to do. When I saw you the other night at the seminar, it seemed that you had been sent to me. All these years I've thought of you, wondered how you were doing. You must realize that our paths never came together again after that prom night."

As she remembered it, the very next day she had been sent to her aunt's summer home on Cape Cod. Martha's Vineyard, to be exact. That summer she made new friends—spent her time playing tennis, swimming, learning to sail, and talking with kids from other parts of the country down at "The Inkwell," that part of the beach where folks of color met. When she returned home in the fall, it was off again to Boston University. She had not seen or heard of Dayton Clark until a few nights ago. She often had a fleeting thought of him and their fateful episode, but she never mentioned him. Nor did anyone else.

Dayton's voice penetrated her mind as she heard him continue to talk.

"My folks were embarrassed and upset. My dad especially. He thought it was all because we came from a poor part of town. You know, we were much worse off than your folks. I mean, your dad was a high school principal, and all my dad had was that beat-up gym."

Dayton's eyes narrowed in memory. Simone could feel his recalled humiliation and hear it in his voice now.

"Dad always hoped to have a big-time boxer come out of his gym. Never happened. He's spent his life in that sweaty, liniment-smelling atmosphere, never realizing his dream of a national champion."

"How are your folks, Dayton?" Simone asked, hoping to get him back on track.

"Doing well, doing well."

"That's good. Glad to hear that."

"But back to us, Simone. It was not right that we never got to say goodbye...to bring our relationship to a proper close. We were jerked around like puppets on a string."

"Dayton, I hear what you're saying, but we were just kids and, well, I'm sorry, and I know it was a mistake. I thought we were so grown up, but what did we know? Later I felt bad about it."

Guilt over her manipulation of Dayton—and that's what it was—tugged at her mind. Now she had to pay for her immature impulsiveness. How could she have been so insensitive, so selfish, so willing to tamper with someone else's feelings? She didn't like the picture. It was time to change.

Dayton's voice grew somber as he quietly said, "I knew...knew that I loved you—and, Simone, I've never stopped loving you. After all these years, all the girls I've dated, it's only been you."

He reached across the table for her hand.

"Forgive me for any trouble I've caused you, Mone, but I had to tell you."

"It's all right, Dayton."

Simone pulled her hand from his grasp and buttered a warm scone. Her stomach rumbled, and she felt a little lightheaded. She chewed slowly on the scone and took several sips of the hot tea before she looked at Dayton.

"Dayton, you know I'm a married woman, and I love my husband. There's nothing between you and me, you know that."

She pushed on, anxious to rid herself of the unpleasant memory of her own behavior, and focused on Dayton. She wanted to see if she could understand him better. She changed the subject in an attempt to do so.

"What do you do at EE&R, your computer company?" she asked as she took a bite of her scone. The waiter hovered by to check if they wanted another pot of hot tea. Dayton waved him off with, "Not just yet, perhaps later."

The waiter nodded and moved away.

From somewhere in the back of the room Simone heard the soft, unobtrusive glissando of harp music. Here in this quiet, peaceful room, she was aware of feeling disquieted and worried. How could she put an end to this nightmare and concentrate on her fragile relationship with Tony, her husband? What *should* she or *could* she say to Dayton to send him back to California and out of her life? He seemed to be looking for some way to heal the hurt he sustained with what he thought of as rejection by her family. Deep in her heart, Simone knew her father had really done what was best for both youngsters, and she could not understand Dayton's unhealthy obsession.

She heard Dayton say something about his company.

"Evans, Engret, and Rogers is one of the oldest black-owned computer companies in Silicon Valley," he was saying. "I work in personnel. Training, hiring, firing, employment practices, policies, and all employee planning come under my umbrella, so to speak."

Simone noticed that the timbre of Dayton's voice had changed. He seemed eager and proud as she listened to him.

"We have about five hundred employees in various departments. We offer excellent benefits: hospital, sick benefits, even paternity leave for new fathers."

"Sounds good."

"Well, it is. We give credit in hours off for employees who wish to improve skills, and we offer not only on-the-job training, but we encourage our employees to further their formal education."

"Do you find it hard to keep employees?"

"Oh no, our turnover is low, I'm happy to say. I'm somewhat responsible for that."

"How come?" Simone wanted to know.

"Well, I designed a pre-employment interview sheet that we use."

"What does that tell you?"

"It lets us know what the employee wants, what he expects to get from the company. For example, we ask the employee to think where he might be five years down the road, financially and otherwise. Then we show him how those personal goals can be reached by staying with EE&R."

"In other words, the employee makes an emotional investment with the company."

"Exactly."

"Dayton, it seems to me that you are doing all right. When will you be going back?"

"I have a few days of time left. I'll probably leave at the end of the week."

Simone folded her napkin and pushed back her chair.

"I'm glad we had this talk, and you know I wish you only the best."

Dayton was pulling some bills out of his wallet, which he placed on the check the waiter had left.

He leaned over the table and gave Simone a soft peck on her cheek before she could escape the gesture.

"By the way, Dayton, did you go to Brookline last night?" she asked him.

"Me? No, I came right back here to the hotel after I left your place. Why?"

"No matter, just wondered."

Who had been watching her?

CHAPTER XIX

From her quiet observations and brief conversational snatches she had had with Simone, Connie, her secretary, was acutely aware that some serious problems had surfaced in her employer's life.

There had been no bantering, no girl talk; even more disturbing, there had been no new business talk. But Connie kept her counsel, knowing that when Simone was ready, she would bounce back. In the meantime, Connie did her work.

Today, for example, she had followed Simone's previous instructions on the organization of a portfolio for Brigadier General Mercer. She had just placed it on Simone's desk when Simone returned to the office after her meeting with Dayton Clark.

Simone started to her office and turned with a weary face to Connie as she neared the door

"Connie, please hold any calls. I'm going to be busy..."

The secretary held up her hand. "Just two things...first, your husband called to say he's picking you up for dinner tonight, and the other is, you didn't forget that General Mercer is due in tomorrow? His folder is on your desk."

Simone struck her forehead with her hand in annoyance. "Thanks, Connie, I did forget."

"Well, I did the research you asked for and set everything up in your usual format."

"Great. Just great," Simone sighed and slid one foot from her shoe to rub her toes along the instep of the other foot. "I've been so frazzled lately, but I think now everything is going to work out. Thanks for reminding me about it. I'll check it over but knowing you, it's probably perfect."

Simone went into her office and sank wearily into her desk chair. She shrugged off both shoes and pulled the russet-colored folder closet. Her name was printed on the cover in gold letters.

Simone Harper-Housner
Financial Consultant
Retirement Frnancial Plan
Prepared for Brigadier General Mercer

Before she opened it for review, she closed her eyes. The tumultuous past few days had drained and exhausted her. Now, she wished she was in Vermont in the ski lodge with Tony, the man she loved. *My life has got to move in a different direction or I'm lost,* she thought. If only she could fast forward the next few days be free of anxiety, problems, and crises. What she wouldn't give to be with Tony, to surrender to his loving embrace, to abandon and leave behind all the annoyances of the past. How she longed to be in those strong arms that would shield her from uncertainties—arms that would support her, keep her from harm. How much she wanted to lay her head on his strong chest and listen to his reassuring heartbeat beneath her ear. She ached to feel his powerful, virile, masculine body close to her own. Today, after the scene with Dayton, she needed more than ever to experience the exquisite delight of his caresses. She recognized in herself the misery of discontent at not being with Tony. In their goodness, would the gods ever permit that happiness to return to her? She recognized the change in herself; no longer self-centered, she needed to share. Wasn't that what her mother had told her?

Resignedly, she opened the folder. It was her intent to offer the general a retirement plan that would minimize the effects of inflation and limit any impact if the stock market should go down. The general expected to receive a sizable lump sum on retirement, and he owned a substantial amount in government bonds.

In the plan before her, Simone had suggested that he diversify and put some of his lump sum into stocks, some into mutual funds, some in money market funds of the highest quality, and some in closed-end funds in Europe and Southeast Asia. Her rationale, she would point out to him when they met the next day, was that growth in other countries might overtake growth in the United States.

In addition, she proposed that he interest himself in the new markets opening in Africa, particularly South Africa, now that Nelson Mandela was its president. She planned to suggest that he buy additional treasury bonds as well. The general had indicated that after a few months' vacation, he would take on a part-time teaching position in a nearby university.

Connie had prepared the outline well, with earmarked funds for each offering. Simone was satisfied with it.

She closed the folder, put it in her desk drawer, and took a deep breath. She had to review the day's events.

On a pad she wrote down brief excerpts of her conversation with Dayton so that she could share them with Mr. McRichards. The lawyer had been right. Dayton *didn't* have any new evidence about their annulment. And for a mature man who seemed in control of other areas of his life, his need to end their relationship in "another way" didn't really make sense. Somehow she had the idea that he had not been totally honest with her. There was something else. Oh, you're being stupid, she thought.

Simone was not being stupid, but she would have been very worried if she had really known what was in Dayton's mind.

He felt justified in his thinking. Hadn't Simone come to ***him*** at the hotel? Hadn't she accepted his reason for being in Boston? Hadn't she had tea with him? Hadn't she asked about his work—shown interest in him? She cared. She really did care. Hadn't she allowed him to kiss her on the cheek? He couldn't wait to check with the detective he had hired. Somehow, in his paranoid, obsessive thinking, Dayton knew he would have to prove to Simone that she had the wrong husband. He knew he could do it.

Since his first job in a mental hospital, Ralph Hohlman had never asked too many questions of anyone. He became a listener. It was what he did best. He got a job as a nurse's aide in a psychiatric hospital when he was eighteen, right out of high school. That's where he learned how important it was to listen.

"When you take care of loonies," he would say, "you have to really hear where they're comin' from, 'n figure out what they're thinkin' 'n feelin'."

He learned some other things, too; nursing skills such as taking a blood pressure, temperature, and pulse. But it was the listening techniques and learning how to handle patients when they went "ape," as he called it, that helped him when he left the hospital and joined the police force.

Now that was the work Ralph loved. That is, until the night he became injured. He hurt his back trying to help a fellow officer handcuff a 300-pound circus roustabout who had resisted arrest. Even his hospital experience did not remedy that night. As a result, Ralph had to leave the department with a permanent physical disability, an injured back.

He supplemented the disability payment with his work as a private investigator. Good thing he had honed up his listening skills. And his days of dealing with crazy, sick people came in handy, as well.

But he had never had an African-American client until Dayton Clark walked into his office. He was surprised to see the black man standing in the doorway a man of about thirty, tall, well-dressed, with a look of intense anxiety on his face.

Ralph thought the guy might be a stage actor or a musician. There were always theatre people around that part of Boston. When Dayton spoke, a mixture of a soft Southern drawl with an unmistakable California flavor, the detective knew the man was not a native Bostonian.

Dayton explained his need for the services of an investigator. He wanted someone to follow his wife.

Ralph spit out a bit of broken peanut shell that had stuck to his upper lip. He was always eating peanuts. Kept a bag of unshelled peanuts on his desk, like that one President and his jelly beans. He constantly brushed bits of broken shells and peanut skins from his clothing and his short bristle mustache.

"What do ya mean? Keep track of ya wife? She cheatin' on ya?"

Ralph indicated a chair beside his desk. Dayton sat down and folded his overcoat on his lap before he answered. He looked around the room suspiciously, as if someone might hear, then cleared his throat and leaned toward Ralph.

"What I want," he said, his voice low and measured, "what I want to know, mainly, is where she goes at night. I know where she works," Dayton told him. "It's after work that I want to know about."

"Doesn't come home, eh? Got a boyfriend in the picture?"

"Not a boyfriend, a husband."

"You said you were the husband."

"I am."

"Oh," Ralph leaned back in his chair as he looked at his prospective client. Sometime was wrong.

"Oh," he said again. "So this is a bigamy case we're lookin' at?"

"Well, sort of...I guess."

Ralph noted the furtive looks his client kept making around the room. He thought, *This guy really needs a lawyer, but any money I can get out of this will be in my pocket first. Then I'll advise him to see a lawyer. Maybe refer him to Miles Blanchard. He'll give me a piece of change for my referral.*

"Okay. Then you want to know where the lady goes at night."

He reached into his middle drawer and pulled out a sheet of paper with some printing on it. In order to save money, he used preprinted contracts and just filled in the blank spaces as needed. He spit out another peanut skin and ran his tongue around inside his mouth as he wrote.

"You see," he said to Dayton, "this here's a regular contract. Be a minute while I fill in the spaces."

He asked a few questions—Simone's full name, age, place of employment and, as he filled in the information, he mumbled to himself. He was thinking in the back of his mind, *This could be a big one. I have a idea I might get enough for that down payment for Vivian's car.* His wife had been pestering him for weeks for a new car.

He glanced at Dayton.

"Lessee, gonna cost one-fifty a day up front, plus mileage. Gas is high 'n eats up money quick. Be 'bout twenty...twenty-five dollars for travel."

Dayton had taken his wallet from his pocket, and the ever-inquisitive Ralph noted several large bills in his client's hand. He became as excited as a little leaguer up for his first time at bat. This was really going to be okay.

"How much?" Dayton asked.

"Be mebbe four days' work, could be more. One-seventy a day, that's..."

"Here's seven hundred." Dayton interrupted. His anxiety seemed to increase.

"Fine, fine." The private eye accepted the money. "I'll keep a record of all expenses. Here," he scratched a note on a piece of paper. "Here's your receipt for the seven hundred."

He saw that Dayton never looked at the paper, but shoved it in his pocket as if it were a gum wrapper.

The detective started to rise from his chair to end the meeting, then he seemed to have another thought and sat down again.

"Need a picture. Got one?"

Dayton shook his head.

"Got to have some I.D."

"Well, she has an office on Tremont Street. Here's her card."

"Um-mm." Ralph looked at the business card Dayton had handed him. It was a soft, beige-colored card, printed in raised, shiny black letters that read,

SIMONE HARPER-HOUSNER
Financial Consultant

"Yes, Tony," Simone picked up the telephone on the first ring. "I'm fine, Tony, and how are you?"

"Good, now that I've reached you. Oh, Simone, I was extremely disappointed and hurt when I got home last night and you weren't there. Like I told you on the phone last night, I won't have you jerking me around like a puppet! Why did you have to go to Chris'? Couldn't you have waited? You knew I was coming home."

"Tony, I'm sorry. I know I've put you through a lot. It's not you, really, it's my own uncertainty..."

"What uncertainty! You love me, Simone, don't you?"

"Of course. You know I do."

"Well, then, there's no need for *any* uncertainty. We'll straighten things out tonight at dinner. And tonight you're coming home where you belong. Okay?"

"Okay, Tony," Simone agreed, relief flooding her mind.

She heard the emphatic tone in her husband's voice. She realized that she welcomed his positive assertion as he told her of his plans.

She had weathered so many emotional upheavals during the past few days, she found that it was a lovely change to have someone making decisions. Someone like Tony. She did trust him. She knew in her heart there would never be a man who could make her feel as complete, as whole, as Tony did. At this moment his calm, liquid voice flowed into her ear, into her brain, and a secure, comforting feeling of love washed completely over her, leaving her excited and warm. In the pit of her stomach, flutterings and all sorts of loving reactions were taking place. She realized at this moment how precious her love for her husband was. *I've been a fool,* she thought. *I could have lost it all.*

Tony was asking about picking her up. She spoke quickly.

"Can you come by Chris' apartment? I'm leaving the office in a few minutes, and I'll be ready by six o'clock, if that's all right for you."

"I'll be there. At six. And Sim..."

"Yes?"

"Don't you dare make any other plans! Can't wait to see you. Love you."

"Love you too, Tony."

Her apartment was all that Chris had wanted—two bedrooms on the second floor in a small, intimate apartment building in Brookline. It contained a lovely, long living room that Chris had decorated herself. The walls were a soft eggshell beige, except for the window wall facing south, which was draped in deeper tan colors with bits of rose and mauve in the print. The mom contained several pieces of furniture that Chris had brought from her parents' home, including a beautiful wingback chair with matching footstool.

"Chris, this is the best chair I've ever sat in," Simone would say whenever she curled up in its enveloping arms. "I always feel so good in this chair. If you ever want to get rid of it, you know where it will have a good home."

"Uh, no way, honey. I'm keeping that chair until I die or it dies, whichever comes first."

"So?" Chris demanded when Simone came in that evening.

"Oh, Chris, it's been a *day!"* Simone flopped down in the wingback chair. "Tony's picking me up at six, and we're going to dinner. Chris, I'm going home with him tonight. I know you'll understand if I can't tell you everything." She jumped up and started for the bathroom, throwing off her jacket as she went down the corridor.

Chris followed, talking anxiously, "But at least tell me about that Dayton nut! Don't keep me in suspense!"

From the closet Simone answered, coming out with her bathrobe on and holding a shower cap in her hand.

"Chris, would you believe it!"

She sat on the bed and faced her friend. Relief framed her face.

"He didn't have anything! Said he just wanted to see me and, well, sort of say goodbye, etc.…after all, we were separated by our parents, and he thought that was awful, and…"

"Still sounds crazy sick to me. Is he staying around here?" Chris wanted to know.

"No. Leaving in a few days, he said."

"I don't like it! A normal person would not fly three thousand miles to say goodbye. Maybe drop a note or call to touch base, but not follow someone to the other side of the country. It's not healthy."

"You're probably right, Chris. But somehow I feel relieved—glad it's over."

"That's what he wants you to feel. Relieved," Chris murmured.

Chris had worked five years as a charge nurse in a psychiatric facility. Many patients had moved in and out of her care, and she recognized the obsessed patient as one of the most difficult to treat. It could be only one tiny segment of a patient's life. He could be successful and healthy in every other facet, but a fixed delusional belief was hard to budge.

She watched Simone hurry into the bathroom. She was happy for her friend, but deeply worried.

CHAPTER XX

Everything was going well. Tony thought his wife looked exceptionally beautiful. He held her hand under the table as they sat close together on the upholstered banquette. They had a cozy table in their favorite Italian restaurant. There were pots and pots of tall ferns and rubber plants. Each table seemed to be in a private oasis of its own. The waiter had just placed an antipasto on the table, with two glass plates.

"Hungry?" Tony smiled at his wife, releasing her hand.

He served a plate of the salad for her and one for himself.

"Look, honey, let's eat first, then later we can talk. I know we've lots to talk about."

"I agree," Simone mumbled, her mouth full of salad. She sipped some of her red wine and felt it curl warmly down to her toes. She hoped things would turn out perfect for her and Tony. She knew that the past week's experiences had put her through a great deal of emotional turmoil, but now she felt like iron tested by fire. Stronger than ever.

A shadow fell over their table. Simone sensed that it was the waiter bringing their entree. But a man's voice washed over them.

"Simone! Imagine seeing you twice in one day!" Simone jerked her head up and gasped when she recognized the intruder

"Dayton! What are you doing here?" Disbelief and shock drained her face.

"Having a bite with my friend over there." He moved his head toward the back of the room.

Tony looked from one to the other, questions on his face.

"Who is this, Simone?" he asked. "Do you know this person?"

Dayton interjected, sarcasm in his voice, as he answered Tony's question.

"Know me? Of course she knows me. I'm her husband."

Tony bolted to his feet and grabbed the man by his coat lapels.

"Her *what?"* His anger rose up and spilled over them all as he grappled with Dayton.

Shocked, Simone cried out, "No, no, Tony. He's wrong! He knows we had an annulment. Tony, your hands!"

She didn't want any physical blow to come between them. Tony's ability as a skilled surgeon depended on his hands.

Dayton was trying to wrest Tony's hands from his coat. Tony was the taller, but Dayton was more muscular and younger.

Simone tugged at Tony's coat, trying to make him sit. Other restaurant patrons were staring, and Simone saw the waiter approaching.

"Tony! Dayton! Sit down, you two, and quiet down! Both of you!" she hissed.

Glaring at each other, Tony removed his hands from Dayton's coat. Dayton brushed his jacket down and sat opposite the pair.

Breathing heavily, he said, "I didn't mean to start anything, but I saw you come in and, well, Simone," he glanced at her, "you did say that you wanted me to meet your husband. Didn't you tell me that when we were in California?"

"California? You two met in California?"

Simone heard the anger and dismay in her husband's voice. He looked at her, and in his eyes she saw pain and distrust. Christine had been right. She should have told him that first night when Dayton had showed up on their doorstep. Now everything was a total mess! Would she ever be free and safe from the silly action she had taken so many years before? Just when she thought security and peace were finally at hand. She did not want to do it, but right now she had to try to free herself from this burden.

"Tony," she cleared her throat, "before we were married, I told you about my…my elopement on my prom night. The marriage was never…" she stumbled, then went on as strongly as she could, "was never consummated. My father's lawyer managed to get an annulment the very next day. It was Dayton here that I eloped with. We had not seen each other until I went to San Francisco to give my seminar. I had no idea he was there."

"She's right, Dr Housner, not until a few nights ago. We've not seen each other."

Tony was furious. "You don't have to justify *my* wife's actions. Why are you following my wife around?" His anger punctuated every word.

"I have to admit I did follow her to Boston, but…"

Tony thundered, "By what right?"

Simone broke in, "He told me he had proof that our marriage was not properly annulled. You upset me, Dayton, and," she looked appealingly at her husband, "I wanted to straighten it out before I told you, Tony."

Suddenly Simone felt cornered, and the whole situation made her angry. She'd been through too much, endured more than she felt she had to, and all at once she wanted no more.

"Look," she turned to Tony, "I saw Mr. McRichards earlier today. He assured me that the annulment papers were proper, and that whatever Dayton *thought* he had was of no consequence."

"You saw our lawyer?" Tony asked, scarcely believing his ears. "Why didn't you tell me?"

"That's right. I saw him early this morning. I was about to tell you when…when he…" she pointed to Dayton. "Dayton Clark, you know I'm right! There is nothing between us! Never was and never will be!"

She paused to get her breath and glared at her adversary. "So I'm not about to be pulled around by you, Dayton, and any sick teenaged ideas you might have. Okay?" She focused her attention first to one, then to the other. "Now listen, you two, this is not the way to settle this. To be honest, there's nothing to settle."

She paused and took a deep breath before she resumed. "Dayton, why do you refuse to recognize the facts? The truth is, I was never your wife, and you know it!"

From his position on the other side of the table, Dayton shifted his eyes from Simone to Tony, as if assessing their reactions. Simone glared at him. Tony watched with concern, trying to figure out what he should do about the situation. He was upset at finding himself in such an embarrassing fix—and, yes, he had great concern for his wife. He wanted somehow to support her position, and he started to speak, but her actions stopped him. The anger and irritation that he heard in her quick choppy sentences, and her rapid facial changes—first a frown, then a scowl—made it apparent that she was very angry.

Tony had to admire the fashion in which she dove into the center of the problem. She had already diffused the situation. Each of them had relaxed, a little.

Simone continued to speak, "Let me tell you one more thing." She punctuated her words by pointing her finger at Dayton.

"I will not, I repeat, *will not,* be embarrassed any further by an error I made when I was young. I agree to that, an error in judgment."

Dayton started to speak, but Simone had not finished.

"Honey," she added, a sarcastic tone in her voice, "that's all it was! A mistake I made because I was young and foolish. But let me tell you something, the world never stopped turning because of that!"

Her long earrings danced crazily around as she continued to shake her head in denial.

"So look, man," she addressed Dayton, not letting him interrupt her, her voice lowered by her intense anger, "I'm going to say this one last time. Don't ever bother me or my husband with any more of this stuff! Understood?" she asked. There was no mistaking her anger.

She raised her eyebrows and threw a questioning look at him.

"If you persist in bothering either my husband or me, you will have to deal with our lawyer!"

The two men looked at each other. Tony shrugged his shoulders as Dayton rose from his seat. Tony stood up, too.

Dayton walked away from the table and out of the restaurant. He did not look back at the couple whose meal and lives he had disturbed.

Tony summoned the waiter.

"We will take our check, please."

"But you haven't had dinner, sir."

"We were interrupted, and our evening has been somewhat ruined, so we're leaving."

"Sorry, sir. Please come back another time. I'll get your check."

It was a silent ride home in Tony's car. A ruined homecoming, Simone thought. Tony must think her some type of idiot. *Can't blame him if he never trusts me again,* she thought. *Well, Simone, you must admit, you were not very smart at all.* Could she make it up to Tony?

She glanced at him sitting beside her, busy negotiating the turns and twists of Boston's circuitous, dark streets. *He must be really angry with me.* The quiet in the car intensified the emotion each felt. Suddenly, Tony put his hand on Simone's knee and squeezed it lightly.

"Honey, don't you worry. If tonight is the worst thing that's going to happen to us, I'm not concerned. We're going to do just fine."

"You mean that, Tony? I know now I should have told you, but I thought I could handle it, clear it up, and then..." her voice trailed off in the dark.

"I know one thing, my love," Tony grinned at her. "You do know how to put a person in his place and with dispatch, too."

"Tony, do you think he can bother us?"

"Gosh, no. I trust McRichards. I just think Dayton, what's his last name..."

"Clark."

"I just think Dayton Clark is a little mixed up. I detected a tinge of paranoia, but I believe two things may help."

"What's that?"

"Well, one, he knows our lawyer is aware of the problem."

"And the other?" she asked.

Tony laughed, and Simone felt relief at the sound.

"The other is the practical, straight-from-the-hip way you told him to butt out. Many psychiatrists say the only way to deal with people like that is with a matter-of-fact attitude that does not feed into the other person's delusion. And that's just the way you handled it. I was proud of you, kid."

"I couldn't stand any more of it, that's all," she said quietly. "Tony, are we going to be all right?" she asked again.

"You betcha, my love. We're going to be just fine. You're back where you belong. Home with me. And speaking of home, we're here!"

He parked the car in front of the brownstone, shut off the ignition, and pulled the key out.

"Before we go in, Tony, I have to say something."

"What is it?" He looked at his wife, concern on his face.

"I'm sorry," she whispered. Her eyes brimmed with tears.

In the dim light of the car's interior, the heart-jolting look Tony saw in Simone's upturned, appealing face stirred his emotion. He reached for her, pulling her dose as she continued to whisper in muffled tones.

"I'm sorry, so sorry…"

"It's all right, my sweet one. You're safe now. You're with me, Tony, your husband." He helped her out of the car and reached into the trunk for her suitcase.

They went up to the brownstone together. It had been only a short time, but to Simone it seemed a lifetime ago since she'd been home. So much had happened to her, to her life, and to her marriage. She experienced a tremor of excitement, but it was more than that. It was a peaceful feeling, a serene sense of well-being, of belonging.

As they entered, she could smell traces of Tony's shaving lotion. It enhanced her welcome-home feeling.

Tony walked to the kitchen, and she followed him there.

"Hungry? I could get a sandwich and some warm milk," he said.

"Let me." She moved to the refrigerator and began to search. "I see you do have some sliced ham. Want your sandwich toasted?"

"For me, plain with some mustard. I'll get the milk heated while you're making the sandwiches."

They ate in the living room from trays on their laps. Tony flicked on the television set. The images flickered on the screen.

"Tony, it seems there's only bad news. Please shut it off," Simone said. "I'm really tired. Think I'll shower and get to bed."

Keyed up and nervous, she wondered about their future. She had always been level-headed. She had prided herself on her ability to maintain her equilibrium. A well-regulated mind and self-control under pressure were traits that she wanted to have always. What lay ahead for the two of them? Would Tony realize that she was sure of their relationship now?

After her shower she went to their bedroom and sat on the chaise, still tense despite the shower. She looked at the bed, then at the long narrow windows with soft floral drapes. She noticed the rug, a lime green that felt like cool grass under her bare feet. The bedspread matched the print of the draperies—Simone's favorite print: greens and greys with the gleam of gold flashes throughout. Tony had told her a couple of months ago to decorate the room as she wished. It was to be their haven. The chairs and the chaise on which she sat were upholstered in the same lime green with accents of gold braid. Simone loved this room. Outside, through the long narrow windows, she could see the night sky. It was a dear night, with the stars visible over the roofs of the neighboring brownstones. Bare tree branches swung slowly with a whispering sound as a light wind brushed them against the dark windows.

Unquiet thoughts crowded into her mind. *Is this enough for me? To be here, in this room, with Tony in my life? Is it what I truly want, desperately need?* What had Chris said? "You must realize, Simone, a heart can be as fragile as a glass dish.

Don't ever break Tony's heart. Remember, the damage will be to your own heart as well."

Simone knew that the moment to decide had come. *Will I go to that bed with my husband and begin the rest of my life?*

As she sat miserable and huddled on the chaise, she thought about Tony. He had been patient with her, and he had been proud of her accomplishments. "My little wife, not just summa cum laude," he'd say. "My smart, clever lady," he would tell his friends. And she was proud of him—proud of the tender care that he gave to his patients, sometimes giving more than expected. He studied, read, and researched, looking for the key to find happiness for others, for a child of their own. She knew that he attracted other women. It was one of the hazards of being a doctor's wife. Remember, her mind said to her, he chose you.

Tony walked into the room, bringing with him the clean, crisp smell of a freshly showered body. She sat on the foot of the chaise; his nearness shook her from her reverie. His bathrobe was open at his neck, and in the glow from the window Simone could see his bare chest with curly black hair exposed. She trembled with the memory of that silky hair beneath her fingers. The desire to touch her husband's clean, warm skin rose strongly in her.

"Simone," Tony's voice was throaty and hoarse with emotion, "I love you. I have never loved another woman the way I love you. Oh, sure, I've had other loves, but none ever matched this love I have for you. You know that, don't you?"

In the darkness, he saw Simone's head go up and down as she nodded.

"Will you think of tonight as our first night?" he pleaded. "Please, my love, the first night for the rest of our lives?"

From the light of the window, Simone saw the emotion in her husband's face. What she also saw in his eyes validated his words. The nearness of his long, lean body sparked a hunger in her own. The past weeks of wrangling and emotional mistrust fell away. In this moment, she realized that her needs could never be answered in any other way, by any other man.

Tony leaned forward and kissed her softly on her lips. His breath quickened as he searched for her tongue. Simone responded with passions that she had pushed back weeks ago in an attempt to extinguish them. Tonight she could not control the feelings; unleashed, they inflamed her body. She reached for Tony's head to hold his face as dose as possible to hers. Her robe slipped open, and Tony's hands slid over her silk nightgown with purpose and intent. She moved closer to him with a movement that gave no doubt as to her needs.

Tony twisted her robe from her shoulders and carried his wife to their bed. In the warm glow of the room, they clung to each other

Tony's voice was quiet. "My own sweet love," he murmured as he kissed her lips, cheeks, and neck. "Tell me you need me, you want me...tell me, tell me..." he begged.

Simone answered with mewling sounds as Tony moved his hands and lips over the sensitive areas of her body.

With a twist he pulled her nightgown down from her shoulders, exposing the twin peaks of her rosy-brown breasts. He groaned with pleasure as he took them each by turn in his mouth.

Simone's body propelled her to the brink of ecstasy as Tony threw aside his robe and gathered her in his arms.

"You're mine. All mine. I need you," he whispered into the cleft of her breasts.

Simone, in a joyous frenzy for fulfillment, arched her hips against her husband until she felt the bold thrust that carried them both to sensations that burst into feelings of unspeakable bliss. Their goal had been sought and reached in a union of passionate grandeur known only by true lovers.

In the dark, their bodies seemed almost illuminated with the glow from their love. They nestled, wet with the perspiration of their spent energy, their psyches cleansed as they returned from their heavenly summit.

Tony reached for the comforter before their bodies could chill. He drew Simone into his embrace, ran his hands down her slender waist, and tucked his hand into his favorite secret resting place between her lovely legs. Simone exhaled softly a long, peaceful sigh. With both arms around his neck, her soft breasts nestled against his chest, she whispered into her husband's neck the words he had ached to hear.

In a sleepy, contented voice she moaned, "I love you, Tony. So glad to be home."

As she slept, Tony smiled in the dark.

He had his wife back.

CHAPTER XXI

Officer Justin Frazier, one of the newest minority recruits in the Boston Police Department, loved police work, especially the Friday night detail. The Holy Redeemer Church in the North End always hired a police officer to escort the priest with the beano money to the night deposit at the bank. The parishioners liked Officer Frazier, and he liked the assignment.

Close by the bank, neighbors and parishioners enjoyed an eating establishment cailed the Venetian Restaurant, said to serve the best Italian food in Boston's North End. Tony and Simone had finally returned, a week later, to have an uninterrupted meal. The priest and the officer were about to pass the restaurant next to the church parking lot when they heard a woman scream.

"Didja hear that, Father? Sounded like it's coming from the restaurant."

The priest pointed. "Something's going on over there."

Officer Frazier saw two men struggling. He waited no longer, but sprinted to the doorway, yelling, "Police! Break it up!" From the corner of his eye he saw another man dragging a screaming woman into a car.

With one hand he drew his gun, and with the other he motioned to the priest to take cover.

The men raised their hands, and the officer radioed for backup. A curious crowd had started to gather.

"Go back, go back inside. Clear this area," the officer boomed in a commanding voice.

The crowd dispersed. Father Camaretta came over and spoke to the policeman.

"I have the make and number of that car that took off with the woman."

"Gee, thanks, Padre. Stick around while I cuff these two. One of them seems to be bleeding."

When Tony and Simone left to get into their car after dinner, Tony had not noticed the men loitering about the front of the restaurant. He felt only a blow on the back of his head and heard Simone's screams before he blacked out.

By the time the squad car and ambulance came, the decision had been made to take Tony to the hospital for medical evaluation. He was recognized at the hospital at once as Dr. Housner, fertility specialist, and concerned activity focused on him.

"My wife, my wife, where is she?" he kept pleading to the hospital staff.

"Dr Housner, she is safe. The information the priest gave was perfect. The guy never got further than one block from the scene. It was a botched-up kidnapping. The police will be bringing Mrs. Housner in any moment now. But let's get you to X-ray."

But Tony was not satisfied. He wanted to know everything.

"The other guys, who were they?"

The two interns looked at each other. One shrugged his shoulders as if to say, "May as well level with him, he won't cooperate until we do."

"Doctor, we've got to complete our examination. You've taken quite a blow to your head."

Tony attempted to get off the stretcher.

Gentle hands pushed him back. The intern spoke. "Some guy named Clark, the police say. He and a small-time private eye apparently had been waiting for you and your wife. When the police got him to the station house and started to book him, he went nuts. Started yelling about 'Mone, his wife.' He went bonkers. He evidently was well-built and unbelievably strong. Took six officers to get him down. In the struggle, he tried to grab a policeman's gun. How it finally happened, no one seems to know but, well, he's being examined across the hall in Room 2. Looks almost certainly like a spinal injury."

Oh, my God, Tony thought as he was being wheeled to X-ray. He could visualize a bleak future for Dayton Clark. No one should ever have to suffer such a fate—no one, he thought.

CHAPTER XXII

Tony drummed his fingers in a nervous tattoo along the curve of the steering wheel as he drove to work. Traffic was unusually light. This made driving to the hospital less strenuous, and he could let his mind drift as he reflected on the past few days of his life.

The Dayton episode had upset him greatly. He felt weary, unsettled, and apprehensive. Even though the study of medicine had taught him order, patience, and the ability to remain calm in emotional moments, now his personal philosophy of self-control and confidence had been disturbed.

Delighted as he had been to have his wife back, the persistent tormenting thought of "what's next" irritated him. Even their lovemaking the night before—indeed, again this morning—had been all he'd dreamed it could be. But still he worried.

Simone had been responsive and loving, and had touched every fiber of his being with her passion and exquisite ecstasy. They had been apart for so long, their coming together had been such a glowing, intense experience that had shaken them both with its power.

This very morning, as Tony watched his wife sleeping, the love he felt for her rose, unbidden, and he impulsively pulled her head to his chest.

Simone stirred and put her arms around him.

"Mornin', my love," Tony had said.

"Oh, Tony, good morning." She had burrowed her face in his chest as she mumbled softly.

"Can you forgive me? All the problems I've brought…how can you love me after all I've done?"

She looked to him like a penitent child, and his heart melted.

"Sssh." Tony had tightened his grip on her, his voice husky with emotion. "Forgive? Forget that…and remember only this: I will love you always, always, simply forever, as long as we live."

Deep yearning for this woman rose from the depth of his soul as he pulled her slight body over his own. Her warmth and the soft fragrance from her skin penetrated his nostrils, and he groaned into her hair. Her reply came with such agitation, such excitability, that it made him quiver. He could hardly contain himself. He had caressed her slender back, feeling the delicate prominences of her spine. In turn, she had settled herself between his legs. He kissed her breasts gently, first one, then the other, as her temperature rose and her skin became damp and glowing.

Tony knew her desire had matched his own as he heard her whimpers of delight. The early morning sunlight filtered through the panes of their window like shimmering silk ribbons, making their excitement and their re-discovery of each other intimate and wonderful. Tony shivered with the memory of the morning and forced himself to concentrate on his driving.

Why, then, was there this nagging apprehension in his mind—even after the glorious encounter of the morning? He knew that he loved Simone and that she loved him. When he left the brownstone that morning, she had stood in her bathrobe, looking like an appealing waif, and his heart seemed to stop just looking at her. He had taken her in his arms. Her eyes were a deep jet-black, almost without depth, with her thick black lashes fringed flowerlike around them. Her skin was tender, tawny-brown with rose tints that made her face soft and alluring.

She had stepped into his open arms and within his embrace had spoken, her quiet voice muffled against his chest.

"Tony, until I went to California, I didn't know how much I really loved you. I've been a spoiled, willful child, not a wife—but now..."

"Hush, no more. Just remember, my love is always yours."

As he continued to drive, his mind flashed back to their wedding day, and he remembered his mother's question, "Are you sure, Tony?" His answer had been a quick "Of course I'm sure, Mother" Did Simone have any other surprises? Would other vexing problems come between them? This Dayton thing could plague them fearfully, if not handled right. Although bright, intelligent, and clever, Simone was volatile—a true fireball—and could reach a flash point quickly. What other explosions were about to erupt? He shook his head again to clear away the disturbing thoughts. Well, he'd deal with whatever came his way. He would make this marriage work. He couldn't let the Dayton incident destroy their love.

He pulled into his assigned parking space in the hospital's parking lot. He turned off the ignition and sat for a moment. He always liked to arrive at the hospital early because it gave him the time he needed to shift gears—put aside his personal life and pick up his professional one.

His secretary was at her desk and greeted him with a smile.

"Mornin', Doctor."

"Mornin', Mrs. H. How are you today?"

"Oh, I'm doing just fine."

Mrs. Hazelitt was cheerful, as always, and Tony felt that she was one of the greatest assets he had in his office.

"I saw quite a few changes as I drove in this morning," she told him. "Spring is coming," she went on.

She got up from her desk and moved over to the credenza near the opposite wall. She poured a cup of coffee and handed it to Tony.

"All along Route 3, soft new-green colors and new life are showing up. Spring is my favorite season," she said to him.

Tony sipped at the hot beverage.

"I know you like spring, and I do, too, but I like winter the best. Think it's the cold days and long, warm nights."

Mrs. Hazelitt laughed.

"That's because you're an incurable romantic, Doctor."

"Could be," Tony mused. "Well, guess we'd better get my day started."

He walked into his office, placing his coffee mug on his desk and his briefcase on the floor. As usual, Mrs. Hazelitt had his day's schedule ready on his desk. He ran his finger down the list. Appointments until eleven-thirty that morning. The afternoon was blank. After lunch was typed in COURT. Ah, yes, he remembered. A court appearance.

He had been subpoenaed by the court to appear in a divorce settlement to give testimony in the disposition of a fertilized egg of a couple, his patients. Each was seeking custody and control over what would have been their first child. He thought, *Why can't people find happiness? Why can't they keep their lives on an even keel?* Then he thought about himself and Simone. Things seemed to come out of nowhere. One had to be ever on the alert for a different set of circumstances.

As he put on his white jacket, Dayton Clark's image swam before his eyes. He remembered the fellow as a good-looking Billy Dee Williams type. But beyond that, he recognized a troubled individual. As he thought about Dayton, Tony felt that he would characterize the man as worrisome. His medical training had taught him to observe, to look beyond the obvious. Whatever the illness, he had learned to evaluate the patient's defenses. Here was an extremely paranoid young man. He had noted that the young man rarely made eye contact, seeming to be on the alert for any insult or potential threat. When Simone had berated the guy for his actions, Tony had sensed an individual constantly prepared for attack, despite his outwardly calm appearance. His muscular tension as he flexed and closed his fists while listening to Simone offered proof of his anxiety. Tony had seen paranoia before. If this guy from Simone's past suffered from such an illness, he was not to be treated lightly. Another concern occupied Tony's mind. Now that Dayton had been injured, would that increase Simone's feelings of guilt? He was actually aware that his wife's sense of responsibility for her teenaged indiscretion weighed heavily on her. He worried that his upcoming trip to Paris, scheduled for next week, would turn out to be a poor time to leave her. Thank God, she could stay with her friend Chris while he was away.

CHAPTER XXIII

Chris bit into her slice of pizza as she watched Simone struggle to cut a wedge for herself.

"So glad you thought to bring something to eat, Chris. I'm starved," Simone said as she transferred the pizza to her plate. "I've been so upset by what's happened these past few weeks, I hardly know what to do with myself. Thank God, I've got you as a good friend, Chris." Her voice trembled. "I miss Tony so much."

"Of course you miss your husband, but why have friends if they can't help out sometimes?" Chris chewed slowly and took a sip of her cold drink.

"Tony enjoying Paris?" she questioned Simone.

"Is he ever! Called me last night after he had done his thing—all went well, and he's going to do a bit of sight-seeing before his flight back. He'll be home in a few days. He always wanted to participate in the International Conference on Infant and Maternal Health."

She chewed awhile before she went on, "I am so happy for him. He was tickled when they invited him to read his paper, 'Aggressive Approaches to Problems in Human Infertility.' "

"I know one thing," Chris offered. "It's good he didn't suffer any ill effects from that blow on the head in the confrontation with Dayton."

"Girl, you don't know how guilty I feel about the whole incident," Simone mumbled between clenched teeth.

Always ready to support her friend, Chris interjected, "Guilty? What are you talking about? You don't have to feel guilty."

"That's what Tony keeps saying."

Chris sensed trouble in Simone's tone. She looked at her friend much as she would look at a patient, trying to elicit some meaning from her friend's troubled face.

"What are you thinking about now? Don't tell me you're off on another track! I can see the wheels turning."

Simone looked down at her plate and pushed her half-eaten pizza around with her finger Without facing her friend, she mumbled, "I'm thinking that...that Tony would be better off without me. I'm going to ask for a divorce."

"A divorce?" Chris blurted out. "I don't believe this! Girl, have you lost your mind?"

Terrible pain showed on Simone's face as she threw up her hands in despair "Tony deserves better than what I seem to be able to give him," she said. "Look at the mess we're in now. Dayton is going to be hospitalized for a long time, and he may never walk again. Because of my past, I've caused all kinds of nasty attention to my husband. The court case and that dumb detective...Tony doesn't need that mess around him. He's trying to build a career..."

Chris slowed Simone's litany with an upraised hand.

"As I've told you before, Simone, you might be a smart girl, but somehow you have a blind spot—and I think I know what it is."

"You do? What do you mean?"

Her friend moved her plate to one side. She reached across the table and grabbed Simone's hands, as if to hold her attention more firmly, and bounced them up and down on the table as she spoke.

"Your blind spot is that you want everything to be perfect. Don't you know that it's impossible to be perfect? Our Lord was the only perfect man there ever was, and He had to die for our sins on the cross! There is no human being that is perfect. Look, be able to ask for help, take advice, and be a team player. You are part of a very special team, made up of you and Tony."

She saw that Simone was listening to her words intently, and Chris rushed ahead with her plea.

"You and Tony belong together, as a team, and you have to remember that. You say he doesn't deserve what's happening now. What he does deserve is a chance to stick by you, his wife. Don't deny him that!" By her tone of voice, Chris dared Simone to refute her statement. "Now tell me I don't make sense! You know you love the man."

Simone answered, "I do, but I can't stand to see him have to wallow in all of the mess that I created."

Chris was exasperated. She threw up her hands in disgust and scraped her chair back from the table. She glared at Simone, and the cords stood out in her neck as she spaced her next few words.

"You—did—not—*create*—it! The sick mind of Dayton Clark created it. And I know that his illness didn't start last month, or last week, but goes way back to his childhood—his being raised by the type of parents he had."

"I don't know," Simone said stubbornly. "I just feel that it would be best all around to cut Tony free."

Chris responded, "How do you know that's what Tony wants?"

Simone sighed and shrugged her shoulders.

"Chris, I know what I want."

"Do you *really* know?" her friend's voice broke with sarcasm.

"Of course I do. I want Tony to have the successful career. He deserves and a good life, and if I can't help him have those things, then the only decent thing for me to do is…is to free him let him find…whatever…with someone else."

"I don't believe you. Not at all," Chris insisted.

She pushed her chair around to Simone's side of the table and placed her arm around her friend's shoulder. She could feel the thinness that she had noticed in Simone over the past few weeks. She hugged the smaller girl closer to her in an attempt to comfort her and squeezed her shoulder.

"Honey," she said reassuringly, "what you are feeling now is remorse or regret—something like that. Don't try to take any guilt. I told you that before for what has happened."

She peered into Simone's face and felt a well of sympathy rise as she saw teats glistening in Simone's eyes.

"Are you listening to me?"

She saw the answering nods come, and Chris thought how she had always hoped to have a love like the one that Tony and Simone shared. She hated to see the distress that had appeared, almost unbidden, on the horizon of their lives.

She, too, had always yearned for a relationship with a solid, dependable man who would accept her as she was and would offer her the "someone-to-watch-over-me" feeling of security and safety that she had observed in Tony. She did not feel jealous of Simone. But she realized a sweet envy of the beauty of Simone and Tony's love. She had watched their love grow, mature, and become a production of rightness—of goodness. They belonged to each other, and she did not want anything to change for them.

She picked up the conversation again, pushing back her own private thoughts.

"Think I'm being hard on you, kid? Always preaching..."

"No, no...I know you mean the best—but Chris, in all honesty, I think I should offer Tony an out, if he wants it. His chance at happiness." Simone's voice came from her bowed head as she rubbed her hands wearily across her forehead.

"Well, at the risk of preaching at you, I still say 'no way.' Happiness isn't something you put on or off, like a coat or dress, don't you know? Look, happiness comes from knowing you've done your best with whatever set of circumstances comes."

Simone still shook her head despairingly.

Chris got up from her chair and went over to the refrigerator. She returned with a bottle of ginger ale.

"Want more?" she offered.

"No thanks, I'm fine."

Chris returned the bottle to the refrigerator and came back to the table.

"You know what, Simone?" she asked.

"What?" Simone raised her head.

"You need to get away."

"Away?"

"Yes. Away. When's Tony due back?"

"By Thursday night, he said."

"Okay. Here's what you do. Today is Sunday. I think you should go down to Richmond and spend a few days with your folks. You need a change of scenery."

"But, Tony..."

"Listen, no problem. I'll meet him at the airport and let him know where you've gone. A change of location will help each of you to focus on the other. That's what you need. No distractions, no reminders—just each other."

"Chris, I don't know..." Simone's voice trailed off.

Exasperated by this atypical show of indecisiveness, Chris flared out, "Well, I do! You're out of here tonight!"

CHAPTER XXIV

Mrs. Harper opened the front door as soon as she heard footsteps coming up the walk. From her upstairs bedroom window she had seen her daughter's husband get out of his car.

"Tony!" She gave the young man a warm hug and led him into the living room. She was obviously upset as she questioned him, "How are you, and have you come down here to talk some sense into my poor, mixed-up daughter?"

"Mother Harper, I'm fine, just a little weary from travel. But how are you and Dad getting along? You look well.

"Yes, I'm here for Simone. You don't know how upset I was to hear this talk about a divorce. You can't imagine the shock when I came back from Paris and heard this nonsense from Chris." Tony threw his raincoat on the couch.

He looked around the room. "She here?"

Mrs. Harper shook her head and sighed. "No, she didn't want to stay with us. Took a suite of rooms over at Tower Suite Hotel, said she wanted to be alone to think things out. I'll tell you something, son. Simone, my middle child, has always been my 'different' child. Never like the other two. Anything Simone ever did, she did differently. She walked at a different time, talked at a different age, even had her childhood diseases at a different time. They had their measles, mumps, and chicken pox over with by the time they were six. Not my Simone! I could never understand how come she was able to bypass her childhood diseases till later, but she was nearly twelve before she finished. Had the measles three times!"

"Simone is different, Mother Harper—that's why I love her so. She is special, as we both know. How do I find this hotel? I'm anxious to get to her." He shrugged back into his coat.

"Oh, certainly, I'll tell you how to get to her, but Tony," Simone's mother placed her hand on his arm as if to steady herself, "Tony, this whole Dayton affair has struck her hard. She feels responsible. She looks..." her voice faltered, "she looks awful, just awful. Please help her."

Even Mrs. Harper's warning had not prepared Tony properly. When Simone opened the door, he could not believe his eyes.

She was so thin. Deep, dark circles under her eyes reflected the stress she had been under. Her usually warm, tawny skin now appeared flat and lifeless. Even her lovely dark hair that he remembered as lustrous and full hung dreadfully about her thin face, the wispy filaments looking as if they belonged on the head of a ghost.

Tony's heart drooped. He reached out his arms to pull her close, but she stepped aside for him to enter. Her voice sounded distant and far away.

"Tony." Her voice was hollow, as if she addressed a stranger.

"Sim! How are you?"

She shrugged and walked into the tiny living room space of the suite. Through the opened bedroom door, Tony glimpsed a rumpled, unmade bed. Evidently Simone had been spending days and nights in that bed, probably not eating or sleeping. He'd have to change that, and quickly.

Tony took off his coat, pulled off his tie, and rolled up his shirtsleeves. His physician's eye recognized that his wife was bordering on a serious state of depression. He'd have to work quickly if he wanted his wife back. He glanced into the small kitchenette, which looked sterile and unused.

The important idea would be to get her back to normal as soon as possible—back to being his wonderful wife, to being the successful businesswoman he had known her to be—back, yes, back to someday being the mother of the children he knew they both wanted. He had too much to lose.

Simone sat, motionless and waxen, in the chair and watched her husband as if watching a television program, as if he were not even present in the room.

Tony found the bathroom and drew a warm bath. He threw into the water a handful of bath salts that he found on the shelf and took a large towel from the towel rack. He kept the lights soft and low. He wanted to stimulate his wife into gradually return to the real world, and not push her too far, too fast. When he returned to the living room, she had not moved.

God, he thought, *this is not my Simone. This whole episode, the sequence of events, her trip to California, the accident, my going to Paris it all has really taken a lot out of her. She's right on the threshold of clinical depression. Okay, Doc!* he said to himself, *work fast.*

He leaned over his wife and took her cold hands in his. She looked at him with questioning eyes, but remained silent. She allowed Tony to walk her into the bathroom, and like an obedient child, let him undress her. He drew in his breath as he saw her thinness. His lovely Simone. He helped her into the tub and knelt beside her. Gently, he swirled the warm water around her body. He used a soft cloth and sponged her face and arms, allowing the water to trickle gently over her. He was attempting to stimulate her senses gradually. He did not want to propel her into reality, but ease her slowly back to the world that she once knew. His heart ached.

"Oh, baby, my love," he whispered, "come back, come back to me, baby. Don't leave me," he pleaded softly into her ear. "Please come back."

He peered into her face. He could see that she was still staring straight ahead, letting him do what he wanted to do to her. There was no response.

Tony continued. He washed her back, her legs, and her feet. He shampooed her hair. He rinsed her hair with water cupped from his hands. Then he helped her to stand under the showerhead. He twisted the dial to "cool" and forced a spray of cool water onto her head and body. As she felt the temperature drop, Simone started to become more animated. She tried to get away from the spray.

"Stop! Stop! Cold!" She resisted and tried to step from the tub. Tony smiled at his struggling wife as he wrapped her in a large towel. He fashioned a towel around her head, turban style, and walked her to the bedroom. He knew that it would take delicate maneuvers on his part to get his wife through this crisis.

As he toweled her hair and dried her body, he talked in soft tones, words of his love for her. Simone permitted him to take care of her. He got her settled into bed, went to the telephone, and dialed room service.

"I need a bowl of chicken soup, as hot as possible. I need a BLT and a pot of black coffee. Please send it up as soon as you can."

While waiting for room service, Tony lowered the lights and put the radio on low. Soft music filtered into the room. He sat beside the bed and took Simone's hands in his. It was all he could do to keep from holding her in his arms, but he knew it was not the right time to do so. Instead, he rubbed her hands and arms gently as she lay staring at the ceiling.

"I'm here, my love, right here beside you. Nothing will take you from me. I won't let it. You're my wife, my dearest love, my soul, my life. Simone, never, never leave me. Couldn't live without you, not for one day, not for one minute. Do you hear me?"

The only response was a slight dosing of her eyes.

Oh, my God, Tony prayed, *help me know how to help my wife. Help me, God.*

When the soup arrived, he spooned it into Simone's mouth. He encouraged her to chew and swallow little bits of chicken. After a time, she brushed his hand away. "Enough," she whispered, her voice raspy and faint.

Tony helped her slide under the covers and saw her fall asleep almost before he had tucked her in. He left a night light on and walked wearily to the living room. Had he come too late?

He'd seen hard work, anxiety, and disappointment drive more than one patient into a clinical depression. Had his wife slipped beyond him? Some people never recovered from such a state. If he could help it, his wife would not be a victim. He would get the best care for her. Would she be willing to seek therapy? Understand her need for support?

The phone rang and he lifted it from its cradle before the second ring.

"Yes, Mother Harper, I'm right here. She's sleeping now. I got some soup into her, gave her a bath and shampoo."

"Oh, Tony," Simone's mother gasped, "you had to bathe her?"

"She was almost in a catatonic state. Poor baby, she's been under a strain, almost too much happening in her life. I should never have left her by going to Paris. I guess the only way she knew how to cope was to withdraw into herself."

"Take care of her, son. She needs you."

"I need her," Tony responded quickly.

"Call us first thing in the morning, please."

"Will do, Mother Harper. Good night."

The next morning Simone woke up, stretched her arms over her head, and looked over to see her husband standing at the foot of the bed.

"Tony!" She sat upright in the bed and looked at him, her eyes bright and dear. The deadened look was gone. Tony took a deep breath of relief and grinned at her.

"When did you get in? Man, what a dream I had last night!" she went on, without waiting for an answer. "I dreamed that you came home, gave me a bath, and shampooed my hair. Wasn't that something? Crazy, huh? How was your trip home from Paris? Oh, Tony, it's so good to see you."

Tony's eyes filled with tears; he could hardly speak. His wife was back, almost from the dead. He prayed silently, *Thank you, Jesus, thank you.*

"Well," he started slowly. He rested his hands on the footboard of the bed for support, his legs shaking, as his emotions swirled around him. He spoke with care.

"I saw Chris when I got back to Boston. She told me that you had gone to Richmond to visit your folks. When I arrived, your mother told me you were here."

"Tower Suite Hotel," Simone added.

"Smart girl, Sim. We're together here in our own lovely suite of rooms. All the comforts of home..."

"Why not?" she grinned.

Tony's heart almost stopped at the sight of her impish grin.

"Well, how was Paris? Did your presentation go well?" She continued to bubble over, her speech tumbling rapidly out of her mouth as she kept asking him questions. "And, Tony, what are you doing dressed? Are you going somewhere?"

That was Simone. Asking questions, seeking answers. She was returning from her own private purgatory. Almost overcome, Tony tried hard to maintain his composure. *Be normal,* he told himself.

"Hey, I just got here. When I told them down at the desk who I was and showed my credentials, they gave me a key. To tell you the truth, my love, with jet lag and all, I am weary." He had already decided to edit his story.

"Brother, you sure look it." Simone answered as she hopped out of bed. "I've got to go to the bathroom and brush my teeth and wash my face."

"Coming back?" Tony wanted to know as he took off his clothes.

"Coming back?" Simone grinned at him. "Of course, what do you think, you've been all the way to Paris and you're asking me if I'm coming back? Man, you bet I'm coming back!"

Tony realized that her catatonic state had gone; the depression had been blocked from her memory. He knew she was extremely fragile and that he would have to be very careful in his relationship with her. Normalcy would be the key.

Simone returned from the bathroom and slipped naked into the bed beside her husband. Tony wanted to whoop for joy. She was coming back to him—his warm, vibrant, unforgettable Simone.

"Tony," she started to speak.

He put his fingertips on her lips.

"No time for talk, not now," he whispered as he enveloped her into his arms. "Doctor's orders, no talk, love."

He tilted her chin up and kissed her warm, toothpaste-flavored mouth. He could restrain himself no longer. He loved her so, and he had come so close to not getting her back.

His mouth wandered searchingly over her face. He kissed her eyes, her cheeks, the sweet hollow space in her throat.

"Tony, Tony," she murmured as she accepted his caresses with quiet moans of delight.

He ran his fingers lightly and tentatively over her rounded breasts and felt her twin nipples rise in erotic ecstasy. There was no stopping him now, and he delighted in Simone's response to his exploring movements. She adjusted her body to fit into his embrace as he whispered loving words of endearment.

He trailed hot kisses along her neck, shoulders, and arms, down to her fingertips. He kissed each palm and the soft areas of her inner arms. Lovingly, with his tongue, he sought the sweet sensitive areas of her sexuality as she began to answer his movements with a receptive arching of her hips.

She reacted to her husband with her own intimate searching. Her hands trembled over his body like a bird's wing fluttering over an opened petal. She sought to savor the taste of his skin, and her feathery-light motions made him cry out. She shut off his cry with a kiss so deep, so fervent, their tongues intertwined so eagerly, that they had to break off for quick breaths. Hungrily, immediately, they found each other's mouth again. This time, Tony reacted with a shudder. Then Simone felt his mouth first on her breasts, her neck, her soft belly, then on the center of her very core. She arched her body again and reached for the top of the headboard with both hands as he continued with feverish excitement to stimulate her. Their rapture continued until they were almost breathless. She extended her hand until she tentatively touched his manhood. Then she awaited his thrusts with her hips raised in acceptance.

The joyful moment passed too quickly, and each lay spent in peaceful exhaustion in each other's arms. Their bodies were rosy and moist, as if a morning dew had absolved them of all their troubled past. They felt brand new and shining, like new beings recently returned from a shared heaven.

After a few quiet moments, Simone broke the silence between them.

"Tony?"

"Um-m-m?" he groaned sleepily.

"I don't remember much of what happened..."

"Just as well, honey," he murmured as he kissed her ear lightly. "It was an awfully hard time for you."

She pressed on with her concern. "I do remember how tired I was, bone tired, and so much had happened, had me so confused. You were in Paris...I...I missed you...besides, I felt responsible for all our troubles..."

Tony interrupted her litany. He wanted to reassure her.

"All that's behind us, love. Don't think about it."

"But Tony, I need to understand, try to make some sense of it. At the time I thought maybe our marriage was over, you couldn't possibly have wanted a bizarre..."

Tony stopped the flow of her words with a soft kiss on her mouth. He looked into her eyes, his voice firm with serious intent.

"Now stop right there, my lady. I love you, you do know that."

She nodded wordlessly. He pulled her closer, rubbing his hand gently along her arms, kissing her forehead, her cheeks, and her eyelids. The warmth of his body and his tender caresses seemed to relax her, and she snuggled against him.

"You're not bizarre. You are a sensitive, lovely young lady who is serious about life and its consequences, and..."

"But could something like that happen to me again, Tony?"

"You mean like forgetting?"

"Whatever, Tony, I can't have blanks in my life."

"You won't, honey, trust me."

"How do you know?"

"Because I love you too much to let anything happen to you. But, if it would ease your mind, we could get some professional help, counseling..."

Simone sat bolt upright.

"You think I'm crazy!"

"Oh, baby," Tony pulled her back into the bed, "I didn't say that."

"Yes, you did! You think I'm nuts!"

This time he cupped her face in his hands and stared intently into her eyes.

"My sweet one, you are my life." He saw unshed tears sparkle in her eyes and felt her whole body tremble as if from a chill. "I promise you with every breath in my body, every beat of my heart, that I will always take care of you. It's not wrong, honey, to seek help. Anybody can have a problem and need some support to take the edge off any anxious moments that might come up. Note, baby, I said 'might.' Besides, I promised you long ago that I'll always be here for you. Come here." He pulled her close.

She looked into his eyes. The truth he spoke was validated by what she saw. She knew she loved this man; she trusted him. More than that the realization almost overwhelmed her he was her partner, confidante, lover, the other half that made her whole. The truth was all there. She would not have to struggle so hard to try and prove anything alone, ever again.

She had almost lost the most important person in her life. Somewhere in the back of her mind she remembered reading maybe in one of her undergraduate psychology courses that individuals grow and develop at different stages. Perhaps it had taken her longer than others to "grow up." But now she knew, with the man she loved at her side, that she could face the world and its craziness. They had been through so much together, but he had not faltered. She was a lucky young woman—and she knew it.

"I love you," she whispered and snuggled, comforted, dose to her husband's warm, strong body.

He grinned at her and kissed the tip of her nose.

"Say it again, baby."

So…she did.

ABOUT THE AUTHOR

Love Always is **Mildred E. Riley's** sixth novel. Financial Consultant Simone Harper is suddenly confronted by a grievous mistake from her teen years. This indiscretion threatens not only her marriage and career, but her life as well. Will she finally accept her husband's love and understanding as she struggles to resolve the set of circumstances presented by Dayton Clark, the man from her past who insists that she is his wife?

"This is a unique story that reveals the power in the grace of love and the blessing of restoration."

—Romantic Times Magazine

2007 Publication Schedule

January

Rooms of the Heart
Donna Hill
ISBN-13: 978-1-58571-219-9
ISBN-10: 1-58571-219-1
$6.99

A Dangerous Love
J. M. Jeffries
ISBN-13: 978-1-58571-217-5
ISBN-10: 1-58571-217-5
$6.99

February

Bound By Love
Beverly Clark
ISBN-13: 978-1-58571-232-8
ISBN-10: 1-58571-232-9
$6.99

A Love to Cherish
Beverly Clark
ISBN-13: 978-1-58571-233-5
ISBN-10: 1-58571-233-7
$6.99

March

Best of Friends
Natalie Dunbar
ISBN-13: 978-1-58571-220-5
ISBN-10: 1-58571-220-5
$6.99

Midnight Magic
Gwynne Forster
ISBN-13: 978-1-58571-225-0
ISBN-10: 1-58571-225-6
$6.99

April

Cherish the Flame
Beverly Clark
ISBN-13: 978-1-58571-221-2
ISBN-10: 1-58571-221-3
$6.99

Quiet Storm
Donna Hill
ISBN-13: 978-1-58571-226-7
ISBN-10: 1-58571-226-4
$6.99

May

Sweet Tomorrows
Kimberley White
ISBN-13: 978-1-58571-234-2
ISBN-10: 1-58571-234-5
$6.99

No Commitment Required
Seressia Glass
ISBN-13: 978-1-58571-222-9
ISBN-10: 1-58571-222-1
$6.99

June

A Dangerous Deception
J. M. Jeffries
ISBN-13: 978-1-58571-228-1
ISBN-10: 1-58571-228-0
$6.99

Illusions
Pamela Leigh Starr
ISBN-13: 978-1-58571-229-8
ISBN-10: 1-58571-229-9
$6.99

2007 Publication Schedule (continued)

July

Indiscretions
Donna Hill
ISBN-13: 978-1-58571-230-4
ISBN-10: 1-58571-230-2
$6.99

Whispers in the Night
Dorothy Elizabeth Love
ISBN-13: 978-1-58571-231-1
ISBN-10: 1-58571-231-0
$6.99

August

Bodyguard
Andrea Jackson
ISBN-13: 978-1-58571-235-9
ISBN-10: 1-58571-235-3
$6.99

Crossing Paths, Tempting Memories
Dorothy Elizabeth Love
ISBN-13: 978-1-58571-236-6
ISBN-10: 1-58571-236-1
$6.99

September

Fate
Pamela Leigh Starr
ISBN-13: 978-1-58571-258-8
ISBN-10: 1-58571-258-2
$6.99

Mae's Promise
Melody Walcott
ISBN-13: 978-1-58571-259-5
ISBN-10: 1-58571-259-0
$6.99

October

Magnolia Sunset
Giselle Carmichael
ISBN-13: 978-1-58571-260-1
ISBN-10: 1-58571-260-4
$6.99

Broken
Dar Tomlinson
ISBN-13: 978-1-58571-261-8
ISBN-10: 1-58571-261-2
$6.99

November

Truly Inseparable
Wanda Y. Thomas
ISBN-13: 978-1-58571-262-5
ISBN-10: 1-58571-262-0
$6.99

The Color Line
Lizzette G. Carter
ISBN-13: 978-1-58571-263-2
ISBN-10: 1-58571-263-9
$6.99

December

Love Always
Mildred Riley
ISBN-13: 978-1-58571-264-9
ISBN-10: 1-58571-264-7
$6.99

Pride and Joi
Gay Gunn
ISBN-13: 978-1-58571-265-6
ISBN-10: 1-58571-265-5
$6.99

Other Genesis Press, Inc. Titles

A Dangerous Deception	J.M. Jeffries	$8.95
A Dangerous Love	J.M. Jeffries	$8.95
A Dangerous Obsession	J.M. Jeffries	$8.95
A Drummer's Beat to Mend	Kei Swanson	$9.95
A Happy Life	Charlotte Harris	$9.95
A Heart's Awakening	Veronica Parker	$9.95
A Lark on the Wing	Phyliss Hamilton	$9.95
A Love of Her Own	Cheris F. Hodges	$9.95
A Love to Cherish	Beverly Clark	$8.95
A Risk of Rain	Dar Tomlinson	$8.95
A Twist of Fate	Beverly Clark	$8.95
A Will to Love	Angie Daniels	$9.95
Acquisitions	Kimberley White	$8.95
Across	Carol Payne	$12.95
After the Vows	Leslie Esdaile	$10.95
(Summer Anthology)	T.T. Henderson	
	Jacqueline Thomas	
Again My Love	Kayla Perrin	$10.95
Against the Wind	Gwynne Forster	$8.95
All I Ask	Barbara Keaton	$8.95
Ambrosia	T.T. Henderson	$8.95
An Unfinished Love Affair	Barbara Keaton	$8.95
And Then Came You	Dorothy Elizabeth Love	$8.95
Angel's Paradise	Janice Angelique	$9.95
At Last	Lisa G. Riley	$8.95
Best of Friends	Natalie Dunbar	$8.95
Beyond the Rapture	Beverly Clark	$9.95
Blaze	Barbara Keaton	$9.95
Blood Lust	J. M. Jeffries	$9.95

Other Genesis Press, Inc. Titles (continued)

Bodyguard	Andrea Jackson	$9.95
Boss of Me	Diana Nyad	$8.95
Bound by Love	Beverly Clark	$8.95
Breeze	Robin Hampton Allen	$10.95
Broken	Dar Tomlinson	$24.95
By Design	Barbara Keaton	$8.95
Cajun Heat	Charlene Berry	$8.95
Careless Whispers	Rochelle Alers	$8.95
Cats & Other Tales	Marilyn Wagner	$8.95
Caught in a Trap	Andre Michelle	$8.95
Caught Up In the Rapture	Lisa G. Riley	$9.95
Cautious Heart	Cheris F Hodges	$8.95
Chances	Pamela Leigh Starr	$8.95
Cherish the Flame	Beverly Clark	$8.95
Class Reunion	Irma Jenkins/ John Brown	$12.95
Code Name: Diva	J.M. Jeffries	$9.95
Conquering Dr. Wexler's Heart	Kimberley White	$9.95
Crossing Paths, Tempting Memories	Dorothy Elizabeth Love	$9.95
Cypress Whisperings	Phyllis Hamilton	$8.95
Dark Embrace	Crystal Wilson Harris	$8.95
Dark Storm Rising	Chinelu Moore	$10.95
Daughter of the Wind	Joan Xian	$8.95
Deadly Sacrifice	Jack Kean	$22.95
Designer Passion	Dar Tomlinson	$8.95
Dreamtective	Liz Swados	$5.95
Ebony Butterfly II	Delilah Dawson	$14.95
Echoes of Yesterday	Beverly Clark	$9.95

Other Genesis Press, Inc. Titles (continued)

Eden's Garden	Elizabeth Rose	$8.95
Everlastin' Love	Gay G. Gunn	$8.95
Everlasting Moments	Dorothy Elizabeth Love	$8.95
Everything and More	Sinclair Lebeau	$8.95
Everything but Love	Natalie Dunbar	$8.95
Eve's Prescription	Edwina Martin Arnold	$8.95
Falling	Natalie Dunbar	$9.95
Fate	Pamela Leigh Starr	$8.95
Finding Isabella	A.J. Garrotto	$8.95
Forbidden Quest	Dar Tomlinson	$10.95
Forever Love	Wanda Y. Thomas	$8.95
From the Ashes	Kathleen Suzanne Jeanne Sumerix	$8.95
Gentle Yearning	Rochelle Alers	$10.95
Glory of Love	Sinclair LeBeau	$10.95
Go Gentle into that Good Night	Malcom Boyd	$12.95
Goldengroove	Mary Beth Craft	$16.95
Groove, Bang, and Jive	Steve Cannon	$8.99
Hand in Glove	Andrea Jackson	$9.95
Hard to Love	Kimberley White	$9.95
Hart & Soul	Angie Daniels	$8.95
Heartbeat	Stephanie Bedwell-Grime	$8.95
Hearts Remember	M. Loui Quezada	$8.95
Hidden Memories	Robin Allen	$10.95
Higher Ground	Leah Latimer	$19.95
Hitler, the War, and the Pope	Ronald Rychiak	$26.95
How to Write a Romance	Kathryn Falk	$18.95
I Married a Reclining Chair	Lisa M. Fuhs	$8.95
Indigo After Dark Vol. I	Nia Dixon/Angelique	$10.95

Other Genesis Press, Inc. Titles (continued)

Indigo After Dark Vol. II	Dolores Bundy/ Cole Riley	$10.95
Indigo After Dark Vol. III	Montana Blue/ Coco Morena	$10.95
Indigo After Dark Vol. IV	Cassandra Colt/ Diana Richeaux	$14.95
Indigo After Dark Vol. V	Delilah Dawson	$14.95
Icie	Pamela Leigh Starr	$8.95
I'll Be Your Shelter	Giselle Carmichael	$8.95
I'll Paint a Sun	A.J. Garrotto	$9.95
Illusions	Pamela Leigh Starr	$8.95
Indiscretions	Donna Hill	$8.95
Intentional Mistakes	Michele Sudler	$9.95
Interlude	Donna Hill	$8.95
Intimate Intentions	Angie Daniels	$8.95
Jolie's Surrender	Edwina Martin-Arnold	$8.95
Kiss or Keep	Debra Phillips	$8.95
Lace	Giselle Carmichael	$9.95
Last Train to Memphis	Elsa Cook	$12.95
Lasting Valor	Ken Olsen	$24.95
Let Us Prey	Hunter Lundy	$25.95
Life Is Never As It Seems	J.J. Michael	$12.95
Lighter Shade of Brown	Vicki Andrews	$8.95
Love Always	Mildred E. Riley	$10.95
Love Doesn't Come Easy	Charlyne Dickerson	$8.95
Love Unveiled	Gloria Greene	$10.95
Love's Deception	Charlene Berry	$10.95
Love's Destiny	M. Loui Quezada	$8.95
Mae's Promise	Melody Walcott	$8.95

Other Genesis Press, Inc. Titles (continued)

Magnolia Sunset	Giselle Carmichael	$8.95
Matters of Life and Death	Lesego Malepe, Ph.D.	$15.95
Meant to Be	Jeanne Sumerix	$8.95
Midnight Clear (Anthology)	Leslie Esdaile Gwynne Forster Carmen Green Monica Jackson	$10.95
Midnight Magic	Gwynne Forster	$8.95
Midnight Peril	Vicki Andrews	$10.95
Misconceptions	Pamela Leigh Starr	$9.95
Montgomery's Children	Richard Perry	$14.95
My Buffalo Soldier	Barbara B. K. Reeves	$8.95
Naked Soul	Gwynne Forster	$8.95
Next to Last Chance	Louisa Dixon	$24.95
No Apologies	Seressia Glass	$8.95
No Commitment Required	Seressia Glass	$8.95
No Regrets	Mildred E. Riley	$8.95
Nowhere to Run	Gay G. Gunn	$10.95
O Bed! O Breakfast!	Rob Kuehnle	$14.95
Object of His Desire	A. C. Arthur	$8.95
Office Policy	A. C. Arthur	$9.95
Once in a Blue Moon	Dorianne Cole	$9.95
One Day at a Time	Bella McFarland	$8.95
Outside Chance	Louisa Dixon	$24.95
Passion	T.T. Henderson	$10.95
Passion's Blood	Cherif Fortin	$22.95
Passion's Journey	Wanda Y. Thomas	$8.95
Past Promises	Jahmel West	$8.95
Path of Fire	T.T. Henderson	$8.95

Other Genesis Press, Inc. Titles (continued)

Path of Thorns	Annetta P. Lee	$9.95
Peace Be Still	Colette Haywood	$12.95
Picture Perfect	Reon Carter	$8.95
Playing for Keeps	Stephanie Salinas	$8.95
Pride & Joi	Gay G. Gunn	$15.95
Pride & Joi	Gay G. Gunn	$8.95
Promises to Keep	Alicia Wiggins	$8.95
Quiet Storm	Donna Hill	$10.95
Reckless Surrender	Rochelle Alers	$6.95
Red Polka Dot in a World of Plaid	Varian Johnson	$12.95
Reluctant Captive	Joyce Jackson	$8.95
Rendezvous with Fate	Jeanne Sumerix	$8.95
Revelations	Cheris F. Hodges	$8.95
Rivers of the Soul	Leslie Esdaile	$8.95
Rocky Mountain Romance	Kathleen Suzanne	$8.95
Rooms of the Heart	Donna Hill	$8.95
Rough on Rats and Tough on Cats	Chris Parker	$12.95
Secret Library Vol. 1	Nina Sheridan	$18.95
Secret Library Vol. 2	Cassandra Colt	$8.95
Shades of Brown	Denise Becker	$8.95
Shades of Desire	Monica White	$8.95
Shadows in the Moonlight	Jeanne Sumerix	$8.95
Sin	Crystal Rhodes	$8.95
So Amazing	Sinclair LeBeau	$8.95
Somebody's Someone	Sinclair LeBeau	$8.95
Someone to Love	Alicia Wiggins	$8.95
Song in the Park	Martin Brant	$15.95

Other Genesis Press, Inc. Titles (continued)

Soul Eyes	Wayne L. Wilson	$12.95
Soul to Soul	Donna Hill	$8.95
Southern Comfort	J.M. Jeffries	$8.95
Still the Storm	Sharon Robinson	$8.95
Still Waters Run Deep	Leslie Esdaile	$8.95
Stories to Excite You	Anna Forrest/Divine	$14.95
Subtle Secrets	Wanda Y. Thomas	$8.95
Suddenly You	Crystal Hubbard	$9.95
Sweet Repercussions	Kimberley White	$9.95
Sweet Tomorrows	Kimberly White	$8.95
Taken by You	Dorothy Elizabeth Love	$9.95
Tattooed Tears	T. T. Henderson	$8.95
The Color Line	Lizzette Grayson Carter	$9.95
The Color of Trouble	Dyanne Davis	$8.95
The Disappearance of Allison Jones	Kayla Perrin	$5.95
The Honey Dipper's Legacy	Pannell-Allen	$14.95
The Joker's Love Tune	Sidney Rickman	$15.95
The Little Pretender	Barbara Cartland	$10.95
The Love We Had	Natalie Dunbar	$8.95
The Man Who Could Fly	Bob & Milana Beamon	$18.95
The Missing Link	Charlyne Dickerson	$8.95
The Price of Love	Sinclair LeBeau	$8.95
The Smoking Life	Ilene Barth	$29.95
The Words of the Pitcher	Kei Swanson	$8.95
Three Wishes	Seressia Glass	$8.95
Ties That Bind	Kathleen Suzanne	$8.95
Tiger Woods	Libby Hughes	$5.95

Time is of the Essence	Angie Daniels	$9.95
Timeless Devotion	Bella McFarland	$9.95
Tomorrow's Promise	Leslie Esdaile	$8.95
Truly Inseparable	Wanda Y. Thomas	$8.95
Unbreak My Heart	Dar Tomlinson	$8.95
Uncommon Prayer	Kenneth Swanson	$9.95
Unconditional	A.C. Arthur	$9.95
Unconditional Love	Alicia Wiggins	$8.95
Until Death Do Us Part	Susan Paul	$8.95
Vows of Passion	Bella McFarland	$9.95
Wedding Gown	Dyanne Davis	$8.95
What's Under Benjamin's Bed	Sandra Schaffer	$8.95
When Dreams Float	Dorothy Elizabeth Love	$8.95
Whispers in the Night	Dorothy Elizabeth Love	$8.95
Whispers in the Sand	LaFlorya Gauthier	$10.95
Wild Ravens	Altonya Washington	$9.95
Yesterday Is Gone	Beverly Clark	$10.95
Yesterday's Dreams, Tomorrow's Promises	Reon Laudat	$8.95
Your Precious Love	Sinclair LeBeau	$8.95

Order Form

Mail to: Genesis Press, Inc.
P.O. Box 101
Columbus, MS 39703

Name ____
Address ____
City/State ___________________________ Zip _________________
Telephone ___________________________

Ship to (if different from above)
Name ____
Address ____
City/State ___________________________ Zip _________________
Telephone ___________________________

Credit Card Information
Credit Card # ______________________ ☐ Visa ☐ Mastercard
Expiration Date (mm/yy) ______________ ☐ AmEx ☐ Discover

Qty.	Author	Title	Price	Total

Use this order form, or call 1-888-INDIGO-1

Total for books ____________
Shipping and handling:
$5 first two books,
$1 each additional book ____________
Total S & H ____________
Total amount enclosed ____________

Mississippi residents add 7% sales tax

Visit www.genesis-press.com for latest releases and excerpts.